THE SPRITE SISTERS

Abe –

with best wishes,

Sheridan Winn

Four sisters
Four elements
Four powers

THE SPRITE SISTERS

THE BOY WITH HAWK-LIKE EYES

Sheridan Winn

www.sheridanwinn.com

THE SPRITE SISTERS – THE BOY WITH HAWK-LIKE EYES

First published in the United Kingdom in 2012 by Sheridan Winn
www.sheridanwinn.com

ISBN 978-0-9571648-0-2

Cover illustration by Chris Winn
Circle of Power diagram by Chris Winn
Sprite Towers map by Chris Winn

For my godmother, Jean

And for Lana-Mae Garrett

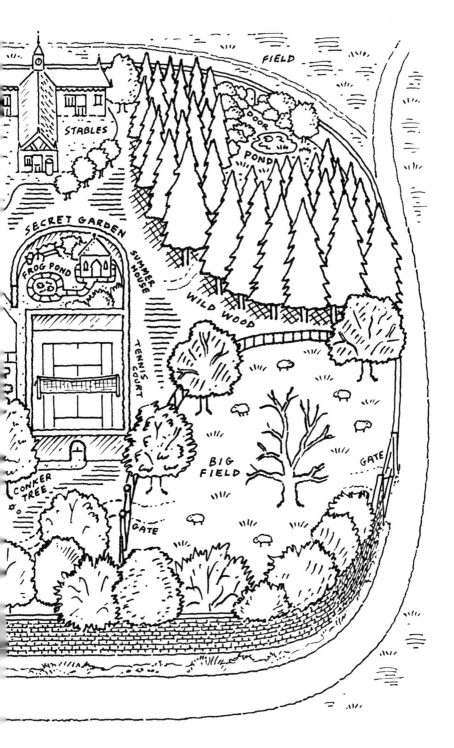

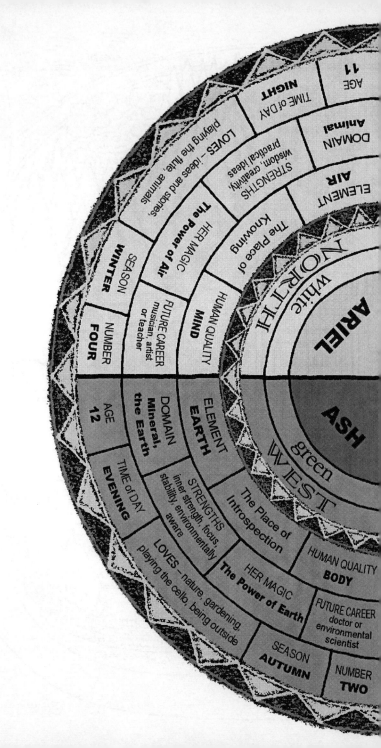

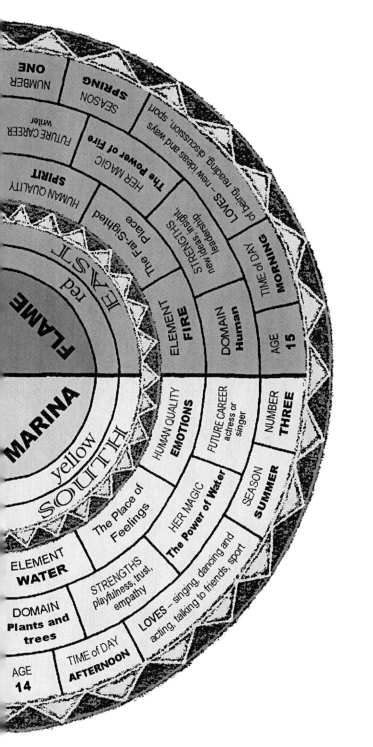

Chapter One
Friday
ARIEL ALONE

The August air hung heavy and hot. Ariel Sprite leaned back against the trunk of the tree, her legs slung over a wide branch. She had climbed high today – higher than she had ever climbed. She loved this tree with its huge, sloping branches and foliage of silvery-blue needles. Warm air wafted over her face and she closed her eyes and listened to the gentle hum of insects. As she became drowsy, the sounds around her began to recede and the face of the boy with hawk-like eyes appeared in her mind.

'Have you ever thought about flying?' he asked her, his dark eyes seeming to see right through her. 'Yes,' she heard herself reply. 'I dream about learning to fly …'

As she sank deeper into her daydream, Ariel felt herself standing on the grass, her arms open wide and her head held back. Then, calling in her magic power of Air, she lifted from the ground. Up and over the treetops she rose, higher and higher, until she was soaring like a bird, moving this way and that through the cool air. Below her was Sprite Towers with its vast, pantiled roof and its whimsical towers and around it the lawns and trees.

The sense of flying was so vivid that it felt real. Ariel lingered as long as she could, but the dream faded. How I would love to fly, she thought, opening her eyes. She leaned forward on the branch and looked down. A long way below, asleep on the grass, was Archie, the family's Labrador dog.

Ariel leaned back and cast her mind to the boy. Quinn McIver, her sister Flame's boyfriend, had brought him round to Sprite Towers last week and introduced him to them all. Zak, he was called. Marina seemed to be mesmerised by this tall boy with his spiky hair and dark, glittering eyes, and Zak had seemed equally taken by Marina. Flame and Quinn played tennis with Marina and Zak. After thundering around the court for two hours in the sticky heat, the four of them sat on the terrace drinking iced lemonade. Ariel had gone to sit with them, despite Flame's protestations that she should buzz off. Ignoring her eldest sister, Ariel poured herself a glass and flopped down on the chair next to Zak.

He had turned to her and said, in a low voice, 'Do you ever think about flying?' Surprised, she replied, 'What, in an aeroplane?'

'No, up in the air like a bird.' Zak smiled, enigmatically, as he said this.

Ariel had stared back in disbelief, then feeling her cheeks grow red, quickly left the table. As she walked into the house, she felt Zak's eyes on her back.

Now, sitting alone in the cedar tree, Ariel pondered on this. What did Zak mean? Did he intend to plant the idea of flying as something real in my mind? It intrigues me, but until he mentioned it, I had never really thought about flying as being possible. It's one thing to dream about something and another to do it. Zak would not know that I have the magic power of Air and that learning to fly is something I may be able to do. Could I harness my power to do this? Is this real, or am I imagining it?

Ariel looked out at Sprite Towers. I have flown above it in my dream, she thought. A moment later, the faces of her parents and her three older sisters came into her mind. She sighed heavily. I'd get mega told off for using my power of Air to try to fly, she thought. I'm always getting told off as it is. That's the trouble with having a magic power *and* being curious *and* being the youngest.

But Zak's words and the thought of flying over the house and garden had begun to intrigue her and the word 'magic' began to swim through her mind, swooshing this way and that. I know I can use my power of Air to lift up *things*, she thought. Why could I not lift *myself*?

At that moment Ariel felt a sharp stab in her fingers. 'Ouch!' she squeaked. 'Blithering beetle bums, what was that?' Wobbling with surprise, she grabbed the branch beneath her and held on, tight. For a few seconds she waited, breathing hard. The tingling in her fingers subsided, but then – ouch – there it was again.

I remember this feeling, she thought. It's my magic power moving through my hands: but why now? I haven't used my magic in a long while. I think about learning to fly and suddenly I have power in my hands? What's happening?

Ariel stared at her hands clasped around the knobbly branch. As the tingling subsided again, she took a deep breath and exhaled slowly. As soon as she felt balanced, she loosened her grip and held out her hands in front of her. Her fingers were longer and slimmer than the stubby pink fingers that had first felt the magic power two summers ago, on her ninth birthday. She remembered the sense of surprise and excitement she had felt then. Now, as her magic power pulsated through her fingers once again, her eyes were wide and her heart began to thump. It's happening, she thought. It really *is* happening …

As the tingling began to get stronger, she flexed her hands. Lifting her right hand, she curled in her fingers and pointed her index finger. It's a long time since I used my power –let's see if it still works, she thought. She gazed up to the higher branches, then down to the lower part of the tree. The tingling was now so intense that it was uncomfortable, when she spotted a hairy green caterpillar, wriggling along a branch. Focusing her mind on the caterpillar, she pointed her finger at it, then gently lifted her hand. As she did so, Ariel Sprite felt her magic power of Air surge through her finger. The caterpillar rose from the branch as if pulled by an invisible thread. For a few seconds, it hung suspended, then Ariel carefully lowered it onto the branch.

'Hey, it works!' she laughed. 'I still have my power!' Then she did it again, this time making a gentle spiralling movement with her finger. At the same time, the caterpillar spiralled in the air. She moved her finger to the right and left and the caterpillar moved with it. Then, as carefully as she could, she laid it back onto the branch.

Ariel felt she would burst with excitement. I'm sure I could learn to fly – I just need to practise, she thought. I've got one more day alone before my sisters return home, but I mustn't let Mum see me.

She glanced at Sprite Towers. Just over a year and a half ago, Ottalie Sprite had learned about the magic power that ran through the Sprite family and which her four daughters had inherited. Fearing for their safety, she had asked them not to use their powers of Fire, Water,

Earth and Air. Reluctantly the sisters had agreed. Since then Flame, now fifteen, and Marina, now fourteen, had become so focused on their social life that they seemed to have forgotten about their magic power. Even twelve-year-old Ash seemed to have lost interest in magic.

We haven't used our powers since we formed the Crossed Circle, two Christmases ago, thought Ariel. I don't think we've even talked about magic since then. It's as if it went away, but magic power can't just disappear – can it? What's the point of having it if you don't use it?

Ariel leaned back against the tree trunk and sighed. Today she was safe from her sisters' interference. It was her mother whom she must avoid. Poor Mum, thought Ariel. She didn't believe in magic power until she witnessed it with her own eyes, and then it worried her so much she asked us not to use it any more. She'll have a real wobbly if she sees me trying to learn to fly …

Ariel's fingers started to tingle again. It feels as if they're trying to tell me something, she thought, staring at them. I can't *not* use my power, she reasoned to herself. If my fingers are fizzing like this, then I'm meant to use it. Aren't I? And Mum doesn't really understand what it is to have a magic power … I want to learn more about it. I'll practise secretly and I won't tell my sisters. I might have enough time to learn to fly before they come back, but I can't practise up here.'

A moment later, Ariel began her descent down the cedar tree. Archie sprang to life as she jumped onto the grass. She stroked his shiny black head.

'I'd better go down to the camp,' she said. 'Mum won't be able to see me from there. Come on, Archie.' With the dog at her side, she ran to the Sprite Sisters' camp at the edge of the Wild Wood.

As soon as they reached the camp, Ariel's mood plummeted and her fingers stopped tingling. Its forlorn air reminded her of everything that had changed between the sisters in the last year. The old white caravan, where they'd had so much fun together in summers past, now looked desolate. She opened the caravan door and peered in. The air smelled musty and damp. The campfire, an untidy pile of black ash, had been unlit so far this summer. Various plastic chairs and a table lay higgledy-piggledy in the long grass. Ariel picked up a chair and flopped down on it.

It's a shame we have to grow up, she thought, putting her chin in her hands. Everything's changed. We used to be so close, but Flame and Marina hardly speak to me these days. In the term-time, they're at Drysdale's till late in the evening. I don't see them as they're in the senior school and when they are home they keep their bedroom doors shut and I'm no longer allowed in. When

I speak to them they don't listen as they're so busy texting their friends. At least Ash still talks to me, but never about magic any more.

As the word 'magic' passed through her mind, Ariel's fingers started to tingle once more. She stared at them, was reminded of why she was sitting there. Flying, of course. A sharp stab ran through her right hand. 'Ow!' she said and shook her hand about. Archie bounced up to her, and thinking Ariel was playing a game started spinning in crazy circles. 'Calm down, Archie,' said Ariel, standing up. 'Go and lie down.' A well-trained dog, he wandered off and lay down on the grass.

Suddenly, Ariel's mind was focused. With her eyes fixed on an upturned chair a few metres away, she lifted her right hand, pointed her right index finger and summoned her power of Air. A surge of power coursed through her hand, so strong that it shot up over her head. 'Whoa!' she gasped, losing her balance. At the same time, the chair shot up into the air. Higher and higher it rose as Ariel found herself stretching as far as she could reach. It was as if something were pulling at her hand. She winced with pain. With a gasp of panic, she realised her power was out of control. As her hand wobbled the chair rose and fell in the air, high above the caravan.

Her magic power, she could see, was like a huge, sprawling mass of bright pink light coming out of her hand. Instinctively, she knew that she must contain it and refine it to become a strong, thin beam. With her feet braced firmly on the grass, she focused her mind on this task – and the more concentrated her power became. The tingling in her hands felt unbearable, but she kept going until at last her magic power became a beam as fine as a pencil, which she could direct with absolute precision. And as she felt this, the chair stilled in mid-air. Gently, she lowered her hand until the chair dropped onto the grass in front of her. Hot and tired, Ariel sank into it. Archie lolloped up and lay down beside her.

Oh blimey, I hope Mum didn't see the flying chair, thought Ariel, half expecting her mother to charge into the camp. Thankfully, all was silent. The tingling in her fingers subsided and for a short while she rested, gathering her thoughts. The intensity of her magic power surprised her. It must be because I've grown older and my magic has grown stronger, she thought.

Archie's ears pricked up as the brass bell clanged outside the kitchen door. 'Come on, Archie, Mum's calling us for lunch,' said Ariel and they ran over the lawn to the house.

For the next half hour, Ariel and Ottalie chatted as they ate at the kitchen table. Of all the sisters, Ariel most resembled their French mother. They shared the same big, grey eyes and fine blonde hair. Both were creative and musical: Ottalie taught singing and the piano, Ariel played the flute and the piano. But where the mother was inclined to be pragmatic by nature, the daughter was dreamy and imaginative. That, Ariel knew, came from the Sprite side of the family.

'Aren't you bored on your own?' asked Ottalie.

'No, it's nice,' Ariel replied, truthfully.

'What have you been doing?'

'Just messing about.' Which was true in a way, thought Ariel. She leaned down to pick up Pudding, the tabby cat, who was winding himself in and out of her feet.

'Do you think he is missing Bert?' said Ariel, stroking the cat. Grandma's little dachshund usually slept in a basket by the Aga, while Pudding slept above in the Windsor chair.

'I doubt it – cats are independent creatures,' said Ottalie. 'Grandma and Bert will be back soon, so Pudding won't be alone for long.' She looked round at the kitchen clock. 'I've got to give a double piano lesson in ten minutes. Will you be okay for the next two hours?'

'Absolutely fine, Mum,' said Ariel, with a smile. She put down Pudding and got up to help clear the table. As soon as this was done, she got a bottle of water and ran back to the camp.

Chapter Two
FLIGHT

'Right,' said Ariel, standing in the middle of the camp. Archie waved his tail in anticipation of a game. Ariel bit her bottom lip, stood immobile, ignored him. How did one fly?

It took only a moment for her to realise that it was one thing to use her magic power to lift an object in the air, but quite another to lift herself. Where should she point her finger? At her head? Her feet? Should she raise one hand in the air like a superhero? Where was the power going to come from?

Flummoxed and frowning, Ariel sat down on the chair and crossed her arms. Then she relaxed, uncrossed her arms and began to consider the Sprite Sisters' magic powers.

Flame had the power of Fire. In the Circle of Power, which they formed together, Flame stood at the east, the direction that represented the aspect of spirit. Marina stood at the south of the circle. Her power was Water, which represented emotions and the human heart. Ash stood at the west, the direction that characterised the aspect of the body; hers was the power of Earth.

Standing at the north of the circle, Ariel's power of Air represented the aspect of mind. When the sisters stood at each of the four directions, they brought together spirit, heart, body and mind. In this Circle of Power, their magic powers were perfectly balanced and had the power to transform.

I have to find all those powers in *me*, thought Ariel, sitting up. That's the way to do it. I have to think about my spirit, my heart, my body and my mind and bring them together in my own circle of power. And when I've done that, I have to *imagine*. I have to imagine myself flying through the air. That's the way to do it.

She stood up and turned to face south, so that she was looking towards the house. Then she raised her arms slightly and held out her hands, the palms and fingers open wide. 'I call in my power,' she said. 'East to my left, south in front of me, west at my right side and north behind me: Fire, Water, Earth and Air. I call in my Circle of Power. I call it in *now*.'

That instant Ariel's magic power began to flow through her body. She felt it as a gentle current of electricity. She could 'see' it in her mind as fine lines of coloured light encircling her body until it felt in perfect balance.

'Now I call in my power of Air,' she said. 'I feel it coming from deep within me.' With her hands still outstretched, she closed her eyes and imagined her magic power radiating outwards. Then she imagined herself rising upwards, effortlessly. For a while nothing happened. Ariel opened her eyes and looked around. Archie jumped up and came towards her.

'No, Archie, go and lie down,' she said. She closed her eyes again and tried to focus on her Circle of Power, whilst at the same time imagining herself lifting. Suddenly she felt her feet rise off the ground. 'Whoa!' she cried, waving her arms and losing her balance. A second later, she dropped onto the grass. That was a weird feeling, she thought, brushing off bits from her jeans. 'Right, let's try again,' she said, as she pulled herself up. Then, standing squarely on the grass, she exhaled slowly, closed her eyes and stretched out her arms.

It took a few deep breaths for Ariel to settle and focus her mind. 'East, south, west, north,' she said. 'These four directions cross at a point within me and that's the source of my power. I imagine this power allowing me to rise up in the air. I imagine my body following my mind and lifting …'

This time she was prepared for the sensation of losing the ground beneath her feet. As she imagined herself floating upwards, she felt a lift. Then she opened her eyes and looked down. 'I'm a metre off the ground!'

she cried out. At which point she lost her balance, wobbled violently and hit the grass with a thud. 'Ow!' she muttered, pulling herself up into a sitting position and rubbing her thigh. Archie ran forward and licked her face. 'Silly dog,' she laughed.

A minute later, Ariel was up in the air again. This time, she cleared her mind and concentrated completely. Whoosh, she went up in the air to the level of the caravan roof. She looked down – it was a way to fall. Hovering in the air – leaning slightly forwards and with her arms out at her sides, like human 'wings' – she wondered if she could move sideways. How would she do that? I must imagine it, she thought. In her mind, she felt herself moving sideways. Her body followed her mind and she began to drift towards the trees – but Archie leapt forward and started to bark at her. Ariel looked down at him and felt herself falling. In the nick of time, she imagined herself rising again and gained a little height, but Archie kept barking and it was difficult for her to focus. I must come down, thought Ariel. Mum may see me from the house. With as much focus as she could muster, Ariel imagined herself dropping gently onto the grass. Again her body followed her mind, although her drop was not as gentle as she had hoped. Another bruise, she thought, sitting on the grass and rubbing her knee. 'Archie you are annoying,' she said. 'I can't concentrate with you making that racket and Mum is sure to come and see what's going on.'

Ariel got up and drank a few mouthfuls from her water bottle. Where can I practise, she wondered. I need height, but I need to be away from Archie and unseen. I could put him in the house, but Mum will ask me why I'm shutting him in. I can't practise in the woods: Mum wouldn't see me there, but I could clonk myself on a branch and there's still the problem of Archie. What about one of the towers? That's a good idea. Archie's not allowed upstairs.

Five minutes later, after she had ensured that her mother was still teaching her piano lesson, Ariel ran up to the attics on the third floor of the house. At each end of the attics corridor was an old wooden door behind which was a rickety wooden staircase leading to one of the towers. Sprite Towers' two round towers rose high above the house. The East Tower was capped with a flat roof and a crenellated turret. The West Tower was covered with a huge dome of glass, which gave it a bright, airy feel. Ariel surmised that if she could fly up to the dome, she would be able to see out over Sprite Towers.

It's a long way up there, she thought, craning her head to look at the dome. Heck of a way to fall. But as ever with Ariel, her curiosity drew her on and within a few more minutes she was hovering in the middle of the West Tower, her arms stretched out wide. It's a wonderful feeling, she thought, giggling to herself. It makes me feel happy to fly. It feels so free! Without Archie to distract her, she was able to focus completely on her magic power of Air.

Over the next hour, she learned to refine her magic so that the act of flying began to feel natural. She practised lifting off and landing. She practised hovering until she could remain in the same place in mid-air. Finally, she reached the glass dome and was able to hover there and look out at the surrounding fields.

She was on her final swoop around the dome when she heard her mother calling her. She must be looking for me, thought Ariel, suddenly panicking. Crikey, what shall I do? I haven't got time to come down – Mum will be sure to see me on the way …

Trying to stay as still as possible, she listened as her mother's footsteps clattered on the rickety wooden staircase up to the tower. Ten metres below her the door opened. Holding her breath, Ariel hovered, as Ottalie walked to the middle of the floor and looked around. She saw her mother shrug, as if confused, turn around and go out of the door. She heard her footsteps retreat down the rickety staircase, then call out Ariel's name again, as she walked back along the attics corridor. Gasping for breath, Ariel swooped down as quickly as she could. In her haste, she hit the wooden floor harder than she'd anticipated and gained her third bruise for the day. Then, as quietly as she could, she crept down the wooden staircase.

The idea of flying at night came to Ariel as she was eating supper with her parents. With one half of her mind, she chatted away to them; with the other, she was dreaming about flying over the house in the moonlight.

'What are you thinking about, Ariel?' asked Colin, with a smile. 'You're miles away. What have you been up to today, on your own?'

Immediately, Ariel stopped thinking about flying and told her parents about the sad state of the camp.

'I'll cut the grass tomorrow,' said Colin. 'We can soon tidy it all up.'

Ariel sighed. 'Thanks, Dad, but we don't play there together any more. Things have changed.'

Her father nodded. 'I know, love – that's the thing about growing up. You can't expect Flame and Marina to do the things they used to.'

'I'm sure Ash will camp out with you,' said Ottalie. 'We'll get the caravan ready tomorrow.'

As her mother said this, Ariel thought again about flying over Sprite Towers. It would be easier to do that from the caravan than try to creep out of the house.

After they had cleared up the supper, she kissed her parents goodnight and went up to bed. As she climbed the wide mahogany staircase, Ariel determined to fly that night – her last before her sisters returned in the morning. Before she settled to sleep, she set the alarm on her bedside clock for two o'clock and put it under her pillow to muffle the noise. Her mother had acute hearing and although her parents slept on the first floor of the house, and Ariel and her sisters slept on the second floor, there were times when Ottalie Sprite seemed to be able to hear a pin drop anywhere.

At two the alarm started to beep. Blearily, Ariel woke and turned it off, then sat up in bed pushing her hair off her face. It took her a few seconds to remember why she had set the alarm. She looked at the window. Moonlight streamed through the open curtains. Good – it's a bright night, she thought.

Very quietly, she pulled on her jeans and a jumper, picked up her trainers, then opened the door and crept along the corridor. At the top of the staircase, she held her breath and waited. When she was sure that no one was moving about she tiptoed down, stopping each time she stepped onto a creaky stair. It seemed to take forever to reach the hallway at the bottom. She crept over the tiled floor and opened the kitchen door as gently as she could. In the kitchen she stopped to stroke Archie in his basket. 'Stay,' she said to him, then she unlocked the kitchen door and stepped out into the night.

With a full moon and a clear sky, Ariel could see easily to put on her trainers and walk round to the front of the house, the other side from her parents' bedroom. In the middle of the lawn, she stopped and looked around her. The night air smelled cool and damp. The stillness was eerie and for a few seconds she listened to the sound of her breathing. Her heart was pumping fast. This is so exciting, she thought, as she closed her eyes, raised her arms slightly and held out her hands. In her mind, she focused completely on her magic power and imagined herself flying over the house. A few seconds later, she felt a lift and rose in the air, leaning forwards and with her arms stretched out beside her.

Up and up she went, higher and higher. Then, suddenly, she was hovering over the rooftop. The air was cold on her face as she turned to look down at Sprite Towers. How amazing is this, she thought. This is magical! It's the best thing I've ever done! It feels like I'm in a dream. It's so quiet and still up here. Everything looks so peaceful. And the house – it's *huge*. And there is the Wild Wood and the old white caravan … And the wall – look how it goes right the way round Sprite Towers. What an incredible place this is … what an incredible thing it is to be able to fly … to feel weightless and to have nothing around me but air …

Now I want to soar like a bird, thought Ariel. For the next half hour, she was completely lost in the experience of flying fast through the night sky. All sense of time disappeared as she dived up and down and moved this way and that. All she thought about was the feeling of freedom, but as she made her third sweep over Sprite Towers she suddenly realised that she was tired and that the air felt very cold. I must have been up here for ages, she thought. She tried to focus her mind on coming down as smoothly as possible, but suddenly the cold felt as if it was piercing through her and her attention wobbled. Instead of coming down on the lawn, she nearly came down in the middle of the Wild Wood. As she dropped towards the trees, quickly she focused her power and swooped up and over them, but the effort had drained her and she came to earth with a bump in the undergrowth beyond the wall.

'Ouch!' cried Ariel, feeling her left foot hit a big stone, which moved sideways with the impact. She felt a sudden surge of panic. Here she was alone, outside the grounds of Sprite Towers, and deep in a bramble patch. Whichever way she moved there were thorns. After a lot of muttering and gritting of teeth, she managed to pull herself up to a sitting position and detach the thorns that tore at her clothing. With her hands scratched and bleeding, she rubbed her left ankle and looked around. Her head was level with the top of the undergrowth.

Close by something moved in the bushes. Ariel stared, frightened. Keep calm, it's just a rabbit, she thought, but she could feel her heartbeat racing. In the trees, a brown owl hooted. I must get back into the grounds, she thought, with a rising sense of panic. As quickly as she could she pulled herself up, but nearly tripped over the big stone again. Carefully avoiding it, she picked her way through the brambles until, finally, she reached the stony track that ran around the wall. She leaned down to rub her ankle again, then stood up and took a few deep breaths.

As soon as she felt calmer, she focused her mind on her magic power. It took a little while, standing on the track in the dark night air, to feel her power; she was tired and cold and wanted to be in bed. After what felt to her a long while, she felt a sense of connection between her mind, spirit, body and heart and at the same time she imagined herself lifting off and up into the sky.

Suddenly she was whooshing upwards and gathering height. Within a moment she had cleared the wall, then the trees of the Wild Wood, and was moving towards the lawn near the house. As gently as possible she landed, sinking onto her bottom. For a few seconds she sat on the dewy grass and rubbed her ankle. Phew, I'm exhausted, she thought.

Ten minutes later, however, having limped quietly upstairs and climbed into bed, Ariel found she was unable to sleep. As the moonlight streamed through the window, she lay back on her pillow, her mind spinning with excitement.

How many people, she wondered, are born into a family that has magic power running through it? None that she knew of.

The Sprites are an amazing family, she thought. Magic had run through the family for generations, so Grandma and Mrs Duggery used to tell us. Not all of the Sprites inherited the magic power and those who had it kept it secret, so that nobody knew exactly who had it and who didn't. Some of the Sprites who had magic power themselves, knew about the other Sprites with power – but not all.

Ariel thought about her grandmother, Marilyn, who had magic power when she was younger; she lost it because she had misused it, but later found it again. Grandma taught us never to play with our magic and only to use it for good. She and my sisters would be furious if they knew I was using my power of Air to learn to fly. I'm always getting told off for being too curious.

Snuggling down into her bed, Ariel thought about Sidney Sprite, her great-great-grandfather. Sidney was a famous toffee manufacturer and built Sprite Towers more than a hundred years ago. He was also a man of magic and wove magic power into the fabric of the house. Sidney's portrait hung at the bottom of the staircase and it was Sprite family tradition that everyone said goodnight to him as they passed by on their way up to bed. To Ariel, however, the ghost of her great-great-grandfather talked back, which had long been a source of amusement to her sisters.

As Ariel's mind began to unwind, she thought about Violet Duggery, Sidney Sprite's niece. Mrs Duggery had the most powerful magic of all the Sprites. When she died last year, aged over one hundred years, they had all been very sad. Yawning, Ariel remembered how the tiny old lady with her lilac knitted hat and big brown boots had clumped into their lives. The Sprite Sisters had been nervous of Mrs Duggery's piercing eyes and sharp tongue, until they realised that she was helping to protect them and teaching them to use their power. She taught us to be resourceful and self reliant, remembered Ariel, yawning again.

As she sank further into sleep, Ariel pictured Mrs Duggery standing on the roof of Sprite Towers. She had clumped along the ridge carrying a stack of pantiles with which to mend the broken roof. I'm not the only Sprite who's been able to fly, thought Ariel.

Her final thought was of Zak. What will I say if he asks me about flying now?

Chapter Three
Saturday
THE BOY WITH HAWK-LIKE EYES

When she woke next morning, Ariel realised she was still wearing her jeans. So tired had she been after her night flight that she had forgotten to undress and put on her pyjamas. For a few minutes she lay there thinking about her flight, and how she had lost her focus and ended up beyond the wall. Her left ankle ached, and as she pulled up her leg to rub it she remembered hitting a big stone as she landed in the bramble patch. Pulling herself up, she sat on the edge of her bed and put her feet on the carpet. Her ankle was sore and bruised, but she found that she could put her weight on it and stand up. A few minutes later, after she had showered and pulled on some fresh clothes, she walked carefully down the stairs.

The house was completely quiet, but it would only be for a short while. Ariel remembered her mother was collecting her sisters. In the kitchen, she got herself some breakfast. Through the open window came the sound of the mower: her father was cutting the lawn. For the next ten minutes, she sat at the table drinking apple juice and munching a large bowl of muesli with a sliced banana.

As she ate, Ariel thought about her magic power. Did she really fly above the house? Was it just a dream? No, it was real – she had a bruised ankle to prove it. But despite that, it was amazing.

Her reverie was interrupted by the sound of voices and the front door closing. A second later, Flame, Marina and Ash came into the kitchen.

'So what have you been up to while we've been away?' asked Marina, sitting down at the table beside her and ruffling her little sister's hair. 'Have you missed me?'

Ariel lunged to one side. 'No! Get off!'

'So what have you been doing?'

'Nothing. Just messing about.'

'That sounds ominous,' said Marina, with a grin. 'When Ariel says she's "doing nothing", then something is happening.' She looked round at Flame, who was getting some juice from the fridge. 'Don't you agree, Flame?'

Her eldest sister shot a look at Ariel, who felt herself squirm.

'The camp is in a sorry state,' said Ariel, quickly.

'Diversionary tactics won't work,' said Marina. 'I think you're up to something.'

'Well, *it is!* Dad is going to cut the grass and Mum's going to help me clear out the caravan. Ash, will you come and camp out with me?'

'Yes, and I'll help you get it ready,' said Ash, dropping her overnight bag on the floor.

Flame sat down at the other end of the long oak table, holding a glass of apple juice. Pushing back her long copper hair, she glowered at her youngest sister.

'Why do you always look so cross these days?' asked Ariel.

'I'm not cross, I'm just busy and you're very annoying,' replied Flame, coolly, as her phone beeped. As she read the text, her face radiated a smile and for the next minute she was 'busy' replying.

'Quinn,' said Ariel. She sighed loudly, then muttered, 'Boyfriends.'

'You've always had a soft spot for Quinn,' said Ash, with a quiet smile.

'Sssh!' said Ariel. Ash laughed.

Flame looked over at Marina. 'Quinn says that he and Zak will be coming over to play tennis this afternoon.'

Marina smiled. 'Good,' she said, colouring slightly.

Ariel used this distraction to escape further questioning. 'Come on, Ash,' she said, getting up from the table.

The two sisters ran over the lawn to the camp. Ash slowed down, realising her sister was limping. 'What's the matter with your ankle?'

'I bashed it on a stone. It's alright.'

A moment later they reached the camp. Ash opened the door of the old white caravan and they climbed in.

'Ergh, it smells all musty and damp,' said Ash and reached to open a window.

'Mum says we need to air the mattresses,' said Ariel.

Each holding one end, they dragged out the four mattresses and propped them up against the side of the caravan in the sunshine. A minute later, Ottalie appeared carrying an assortment of cleaning materials. For the next half hour, Ash cleaned the windows outside and Ariel did them inside, while Ottalie wiped down the surfaces and floor of the caravan.

As they finished, Colin drove in to the camp on his ride-on lawn mower. Ash and Ariel moved the table and chairs to one side, then back the other, as he cut the grass. Soon the camp was ship-shape.

'There you go, girls,' said Colin, getting off the mower. 'We just need to sort out the camp fire.'

Ash and Ariel went into the Wild Wood to gather kindling and small logs, whilst their father cleaned out the old fire and laid a new one.

As soon as their parents left the camp, Ash tightened up the rope that was strung on poles and ran around the perimeter. Ariel straightened the sign that Marina had painted two years ago and which they had nailed to a post at the entrance. It read, 'No Grown-Ups Without Permission'.

Ariel stared at the sign and screwed up her nose. 'Does that mean Flame can't come in, since she keeps trying to act like a grown-up?'

Ash came up beside her and shrugged. 'I don't know. S'pose it depends on whether she wants to.'

'Maybe we don't want Miss Bossy Pants here,' muttered Ariel.

Ash laughed.

'Well, she's no fun any more.'

They walked into the middle of the camp and sat down on two of the chairs. Ariel rested her chin on her hands and looked over at her sister. 'Do you ever think about your magic power?'

Ash nodded. 'Sometimes I carry my magic stone in my pocket.'

'You didn't tell me.'

'Well, we haven't talked about magic for a long while. Why? Has something happened?'

Ariel looked down at the ground. 'No,' she said, feeling Ash's steady gaze on her face. 'It's a shame we don't even talk about it any more.'

'Grandma told us we were only ever to use our magic power for good.'

'I know,' replied Ariel. 'It's just – just a shame that we don't use it for … *something.*'

'What Glenda Glass put us through was frightening,' said Ash. 'I'm not sure I'd want to go through that again.'

'But we learned so much – and it was incredibly exciting.'

'True.'

The two girls were silent for a while, each remembering how Glenda Glass, another member of the Sprite family, had been vengeful against the sisters. Using her dark magic, she had tried to take their magic and seize Sprite Towers. After a series of terrifying battles with Glenda, the Sprite Sisters found a way to use their powers to transform her dark magic into good magic.

'I've been thinking about my magic power of Air,' said Ariel.

'Oh?' Ash's gentle brown eyes had a sudden look of concern. She waited for Ariel to continue, but her sister was silent. 'Please be careful, Ariel.'

Unable to look Ash in the eye, Ariel stared at the ground and nodded. Then she jumped up and said,

'Come on, let's get some supplies for the camp.' For the rest of the morning, they ferried down sleeping bags, food, books, lamps and everything else they thought they might need.

Unsettled by Ariel's sudden interest in her magic power, Ash went to her bedroom and pulled out a box from the bookshelf. She carried it to the bed, put it down and opened the lid. Inside was the magic stone: round in shape, grey-brown in colour and flattened on two sides. She had found the stone in a secret cavity in the wall at Sprite Towers and instantly recognised its magic. Since then, the stone had warned Ash and her sisters many times when they had been in danger.

Ash laid it in the palm of her hand, loved the feeling of its smoothness. Tucking it into her pocket, she put back the lid on the box and returned it to its shelf. Just in case, she thought, feeling the shape of the stone through her jeans.

As soon as lunch was over, Flame and Marina changed into their whites and got ready to play tennis.

Zak's arrival presented Ariel with a dilemma. On the one hand she felt curious to see him again, wondering if he would ask her a second time about flying. On the other hand, it was the last thing she wanted to be asked about. Curiosity got the better of her and she hung around. Besides, as Ash had pointed out, Ariel had a soft spot for Quinn and wanted to say hello. She enjoyed his gentle teasing and his kind, dark eyes. He was always pleased to see her too, which annoyed Flame. Often she turned up just as he was about to kiss Flame, which amused her as much as it annoyed her eldest sister.

'Hi Ariel – nice to see you,' said Quinn, with a smile.

She smiled up at him. 'Hi Quinn.'

'Hi Ariel,' said Zak, looking down at her. His dark eyes seemed to go right through her.

'Hello,' she replied and turned away to deflect his gaze.

As Zak greeted Ash, Ariel noticed that she looked uncomfortable under his gaze. Marina, however, watched him closely and with a big smile on her lovely face.

'Close your mouth, Ariel – you look like a goldfish,' said Flame, sharply.

Ariel grinned at Zak. 'Flame thinks I'm annoying.'

'Are you?'

Ariel nodded. 'Sometimes. What do you think, Quinn?'

Flame groaned. 'Oh do go away, Ariel.'

Quinn laughed and gave Ariel a slight bow of his

head. 'I think you're delightful, Ariel.'

'Thank you,' she said and gave him a slight bow of her head.

Flame groaned again. 'Come on, let's go and play tennis.'

Whilst the others played tennis, Ash and Ariel went down to the camp.

'Zak has a face like a hawk,' said Ash. 'Those dark, piercing eyes.'

'That's just what I thought,' said Ariel. 'They seemed to bore holes right through me.'

'He's nice looking though,' said Ash. 'Seems very laid back.'

Ariel sighed. 'Boys …'

Two hours later, when Flame and Marina, Quinn and Zak were sitting on the terrace having a glass of homemade lemonade, Ash and Ariel went to join them. Quinn poured them a drink. 'Thank you,' said Ariel, taking hers. Ash sat down next to Quinn, which left the chair beside Zak for Ariel. Drawing in a sharp breath, she sat down.

As soon as the others began talking, Zak turned to Ariel and said softly, 'Well, have you thought about it?'

Ariel blinked. 'What?'

Zak laughed. 'Flying. Have you forgotten?' His manner was so assured, his gaze so steady that Ariel felt like a rabbit fixed in the headlights of a car. Her mind began to whirr. How could he know? She had been flying over Sprite Towers last night! What should she say? Nothing. Play dumb, she thought.

'No,' she said, her grey eyes wide. 'Why, have you?'

Watching her, Zak nodded. 'All the time,' he said. 'You should try it. Flying is cool.'

Ariel felt the colour rising in her cheeks. Did he see me, she wondered, casting her mind back to her flight over the house. The thought of this alarmed her. I must get away, she thought, for the second time that week. She put her drink on the table and said, 'Need the loo.' As she ran into the house, she could feel Zak's eyes on her back.

She went into the cloakroom in the hallway, locked the door and leaned against it breathing hard. Why did he ask me again about flying? How could he possibly know that I have the power to fly?

Ariel was so thrown by Zak's question and so angry with herself for sitting down beside him that she went up to her room, rather than return outside. She was lying on her bed, staring at the ceiling, when Ash came in.

'Are you okay?'

Ariel propped herself up on her elbows. 'Yes.'

'What did Zak say to you that made you dash off so

quickly?' asked Ash, sitting down on the sugar pink bed.

Ariel looked at her sister. It was almost impossible to lie to Ash: she had such gentle eyes. Ariel sighed, 'He asked me if I'd ever thought about flying.'

Ash shrugged. 'And have you?'

'No,' said Ariel, quickly. 'Well. Yes. Sometimes. I just thought it was an odd thing to ask me. I have the feeling he can see into my mind.'

Ash nodded. 'There's something unsettling about him, I agree. Marina can't take her eyes off him.'

'Do you like him?

Ash frowned. 'I haven't made up my mind yet.'

They were silent for a moment, then Ash shivered. 'I feel like something is crawling up my back.'

Chapter Four
Saturday night and Sunday
EYES IN THE NIGHT

Ariel hated herself for lying to Ash, but the desire to fly again – that night, if possible – was so strong in her that she dare not share her secret. Zak was right. Flying *was* cool. Instead of telling her sister, Ariel pushed it to one side of her mind and concentrated on the job of camping out and cooking supper on the campfire. It was fun to be with Ash, but their camp was much quieter than the camps of previous years when they'd all been sitting around the fire.

Mum wanted them to keep Archie with them in the caravan that night, but Ash and Ariel were adamant that they would be okay and that the big dog would get restless in such a confined space and keep them awake. They would take their mobile phones, they assured their mother. Dad came down to check on them, as he always did before he went to bed. Since Ash had no reason to suspect that her little sister was planning to fly over Sprite Towers in the middle of the night, she went off to sleep unawares.

Ariel waited until Ash fell asleep, but then she

dropped off herself. She woke again in the small hours of the morning. Ash was sleeping deeply as she crept out of the caravan. If Ash woke and asked where she was going, she would say she needed a pee. But Ash did not wake, and ten minutes later Ariel lifted off from the edge of the lawn and flew over Sprite Towers for a second time. In the moonlight, her night flight had a dreamy quality to it as she swooped this way and that, looking down at the house and grounds. She spent some time refining her power, so that she could rise quickly, then drop. She practised turning and bending, her arms outstretched, her head held back.

There was only one blip: as she came down to land, she had the distinct sense that someone was standing on the track that ran beyond the Wild Wood, the other side of the high brick wall. She could just make out the dark shape of someone tall moving along. Had they seen her, up in the air? A shiver of panic ran up her spine. She came down as gently as possible, hidden by the trees. It's probably a poacher, Ariel thought, as she landed on the lawn.

She stood still and looked around nervously. The night suddenly felt very dark and very cold. The thought of someone being out there – close by and only the other side of the wall – unsettled her. The wall is nearly four metres high, she thought. No one is going to climb over it and nor are they going to come all the way around to the front of Sprite Towers. Feeling doubtful about this and wondering what they were doing there in the first place, Ariel walked thoughtfully over the damp grass. As she passed the Wild Wood, she held her breath as an old red fox crept past her. By the time she reached the caravan her heart was beating fast, but she opened the door quietly and crept in, locking it behind her. For a few seconds she stood still and listened to the sound of Ash's breathing. She was safe: her sister was still asleep. Carefully, Ariel pulled off her trainers and climbed back into her sleeping bag. For a few minutes she listened for any strange noise outside, but everything was still. Perhaps we should have had Archie with us after all, she thought, as she drifted off to sleep.

On Sunday morning, Ariel braced herself for some questions from Ash – she felt sure her sister must have heard her leave the caravan – but none came and Ariel relaxed. With Flame and Marina, however, she kept up her guard and stayed as far away from them as possible. Once Flame started probing into something, she kept going until she found the answer, so it was best to avoid her completely. It was not so difficult to avoid Flame and Marina these days, as they locked themselves away in their rooms most of the time – or so it seemed to Ariel.

She was no longer allowed into these apparently sacred spaces. When she did see her sisters, they were busy texting or talking on their phones. If she asked them a question, they grunted by way of reply.

From time to time through the day, Ariel wondered about the shadowy figure on the track. She wanted so much to tell Ash, but if she did, she would have to admit to using her magic power to fly – and that would be the end of it. Ariel was hooked. All day, she thought about flying. She couldn't wait until the night, when she would lift off again over the house and feel the cool air on her face.

Ash noticed that her little sister seemed miles away and that she looked a little tired. What struck her most, however, was that Ariel was quiet. Ariel was rarely quiet. Usually she chattered away, but today she seemed in a dream. Even when they had bicycle races over the lawn, Ariel was not fully engaged. The other thing that alerted Ash was that Ariel's trainers were soaking wet and covered with grass clippings when they woke up that morning.

Alone in the caravan for a few minutes, Ash reached into her jeans pocket, took out her magic stone and held it in her flat palm. When she asked it if Ariel was using her magic power, the stone lit up, confirming her question. So she is using it, thought Ash. I thought there was something going on when she asked me about our magic power the other day …

Ash deduced that Ariel might be using her power at night. That evening, when they shut the caravan door and tucked themselves into their sleeping bags, Ash determined to wake if Ariel did. Sure enough, in the middle of the night, Ash heard her little sister climb out of bed, pick up her trainers and open the door of the caravan.

A few minutes after Ariel left, Ash followed. In the moonlight, she could see the trail that Ariel had made in the dewy grass. She could see that Ariel had walked across the lawn to the front of the house. Then, in the middle of the lawn, her footprints stopped. Where has she gone, Ash wondered, looking around. For one awful moment, she thought something had swallowed her sister and carried her off into the night sky. With her heart pounding, Ash looked up, her eyes scanning from side to side, up and down. The night was clear and the moon radiated the rich orange glow of a harvest moon. Finally she saw her. High above the house, and with her arms open wide, was her little sister. Flying. Ash was so surprised she fell down on her bottom. 'Oh my God,' she said, sitting back on the damp grass. She sat there some while, watching Ariel – who didn't seem to have seen her, perhaps because Ash was in the shadow of the trees.

After a few minutes, Ash stood up and carefully picked her way back to the caravan.

Up above, Ariel swooshed this way and that. Her magic power was beginning to feel more refined, easier to control. This is blissful, she thought, as she glided through the air.

Just then she caught sight of the Wild Wood. Her heart missed a beat as she wondered if the figure was standing there again tonight. Hovering slowly near the tall pine trees, she gazed down and gasped. There was no sign of the figure beyond the wall, but looking up at her between the trees were a hundred pairs of big yellow eyes. Each pair of eyes was fixed on her. There was something nasty about them and Ariel gave a shudder of fear.

Concentrate, concentrate, she thought. I must not fall, I must not fall. Gathering a little height, she moved towards the eastern edge of the Wild Wood. The eyes followed her. She moved towards the west side and the eyes swivelled back, all the time focused on her. What can they be? She flew down onto the lawn so quickly that she landed with a crash and grazed her face and hands.

As fast as she could, Ariel picked herself up from the grass and ran towards the caravan. She pulled opened the door – and there was Ash, sitting on her bed holding a torch under her chin. In the beam of the light, her white face looked like a ghost.

'Oh don't!' cried Ariel, closing the door behind her. 'Don't – please don't!' She fell onto her bed and burst into tears.

'What's happened?' said Ash, putting down the torch. She climbed onto Ariel's bed beside her sister and pointed the torch at Ariel's face and hands. 'Hey, you're bleeding. Did you land too hard?'

Ariel nodded and drew a sharp breath. She pulled herself up, and then sitting beside Ash she looked round at her sister and whispered, 'There were these eyes. Horrible eyes looking at up me.' Ariel stared in front of her and her body began to shake.

'Hey, hey, calm down,' said Ash, putting her arm around Ariel's shoulders. 'Just tell me what happened from start to finish.'

'You won't be cross?' whispered Ariel.

'I don't know. Perhaps. But I think you should still tell me.' Ash's voice was soothing and kind.

Ariel looked at her sister, with her tufty chestnut hair and soft brown eyes. 'All right,' she snuffled, loudly. 'Is the door locked?'

'I don't think so,' said Ash, and got up to close it. 'Are you worried there's someone out there?'

Ariel nodded and made another loud snuffling

noise. 'I saw someone standing on the track the other side of the wall last night.'

'What! Who would that be?'

Ariel shook her head. 'I could just see it was someone tall.'

For a moment, Ash stood still, then she turned the key in the lock and pushed the bolt shut. 'I'm sure we're safe here,' she said, as she sat back down beside her little sister and pulled the sleeping bag over them.

Ariel gave a little sob. 'Flame will be furious with me.'

'Perhaps we don't need to tell her.'

Ariel nodded. 'Are you sure the door's locked?'

'Yes. Please tell me what's happened. I know you've been flying.'

Ariel caught Ash's eye in the dim torchlight. 'You saw me?'

'I followed you.'

'Oh.'

'Did you see me fly?'

Ash smiled. 'Yes – it was amazing. I had no idea you had such power.'

'Neither did I.'

Huddled under the sleeping bag, Ariel told Ash her story. She told her sister about Zak asking her if she could fly. Ash looked worried about this. Ariel told her she wanted to explore her magic power, how she'd found she could fly and how much she loved it. She told Ash about the shadowy figure on the track, at which Ash frowned. Finally Ariel came to the yellow eyes.

Ash squirmed. 'They sound creepy.'

'There was something nasty about them.' Ariel shivered.

'So what shall we do?' said Ash, with a thoughtful gaze. 'I'm worried about this person hanging around, too.'

'I don't want to go out there and look now.'

'No, nor do I. I think we should go to sleep and see if we can find the eyes in the morning. And perhaps we should bring Archie down here, when we camp out again.'

'You're not cross with me for using my magic power?'

Ash sighed. 'I'm not happy about it, but you've done it now – and it can't be undone.'

'Don't you ever wonder about your power, Ash? Mine's grown so much stronger. I'll bet yours has too.'

Ash held up her right hand and shone the torch on it. 'Hm,' she murmured, staring at it. 'Maybe.'

'If I can fly in the air with my power of Air, maybe you can burrow into the ground with your power of Earth.'

'Doesn't sound as much fun as flying,' said Ash, with a grin.

Ariel giggled, then yawned loudly. 'I'm so tired,' she said.

Ash got off her sister's bed and climbed back onto her own. Two minutes later they were sound asleep.

Chapter Five
Monday
SISTERS INVESTIGATE

Ariel woke late next morning, sat up in her sleeping bag and pushed her tousled hair off her face. For a while she gazed out of the caravan window. The weather had changed and huge, billowy clouds moved briskly across the sky. The air inside the caravan felt chilly. Ariel remembered the yellow eyes and shivered.

A minute later, Ash woke up. The two sisters climbed out of their sleeping bags and ran up to the house for a shower and some clean clothes. Flame and Marina were still asleep in their bedrooms, Colin had already left for work and Ottalie was doing some piano practice, so Ash and Ariel had breakfast alone in the kitchen. Ash made scrambled eggs, while Ariel made toast and poured glasses of apple juice. When the food was ready, they sat down and tucked in.

'I'm so hungry,' said Ariel, through a mouthful of squishy yellow egg.

Ash yawned. 'So am I. And tired.'

Ariel looked at her sister with an anxious face. 'You won't tell, will you?'

Ash shook her head. 'No.'

Ariel gave a big sigh of relief.

'But I want you to promise me you'll stop flying.'

Ariel frowned and pursed her lips.

'We promised Grandma not to play with our power,' said Ash. She watched Ariel, waited for a reply, but they were interrupted as Ottalie came into the kitchen.

'Morning,' she said, with a smile. She poured herself a cup of coffee and sat down with her daughters. 'So how was your camp last night? Did you have fun?'

Ariel glanced at Ash, then said, 'It was fine, Mum, thanks.'

'Good. So what are you up to, today?'

'We're going on a hunt in the Wild Wood,' said Ariel.

Ottalie raised an amused eyebrow as she sipped her coffee.

'To improve our tracking skills,' added Ash, buttering her second piece of toast.

'What do you expect to find?'

The sisters looked at one another. 'Tracks,' said Ariel, with a serious face.

'No grizzly bears or aliens?'

Ariel's grey eyes opened as wide as saucers as she stared at her mother. Maybe the yellow eyes she'd seen were alien. What then? The thought of this made Ariel shiver.

Noticing this, and hoping her mother hadn't, Ash said, 'Alien life is *always* a possibility, Mum.'

Ottalie laughed. 'Absolutely! Well, take care in the Wild Wood. You don't know what's out there.'

'We will, Mum,' said Ash.

As soon as the two girls had cleared up their breakfast things and got some new supplies for their larder, they ran back to the camp. Archie lolloped along at their side. They stowed away the food in the caravan and tidied up their clothes and bedding. When they had finished their tasks, Ash and Ariel stood in the middle of the camp looking towards the Wild Wood.

The tall pine trees looked forbidding, even in the August sunshine. The Wild Wood always had a mysterious feel. The sisters knew that once they left the light and green of the camp and stepped into the Wild Wood, all would be dark and silent. Here the trees grew close together, allowing little light to penetrate. Years of pine needles had fallen from the branches and formed a carpet on the ground so dense that sounds in the wood were muffled. The pine needles were so acidic that no plants would grow there and few birds passed through. Behind the Wild Wood ran the high brick wall and beyond that the track, where Ariel thought she had seen the shadowy figure on her Sunday night flight. Staring at the trees, the sisters hesitated.

'Whereabouts do you think you saw the yellow eyes last night?' asked Ash.

'Towards the back of the wood, near the wall,' said Ariel, pointing. 'Have you brought your magic stone?'

'Yep,' replied Ash. She pulled it out of her pocket and held it out in the palm of her open hand. The smooth, brown stone glistened in the sunshine. 'It's not doing anything at the moment.'

'Let's see what happens when we go in.'

They walked towards the Wild Wood and stopped at the edge. Archie bounded up behind them. He stopped too, stared into the trees and gave a low growl.

Ariel and Ash looked down at the dog and exchanged glances.

'Come on,' said Ariel and she stepped into the wood, pushing down a bramble and climbing over another. Ash climbed over a fallen branch and narrowly avoided a rabbit hole. With a bound over the branch, Archie followed them.

In the trees, all was quiet. The sounds of the outside world receded. The girls looked around them, every sense alert. To their right, two rabbits skittered through the undergrowth back to their warren. Archie made a lurch towards them. *'Leave it!'* said Ariel, grabbing hold of his collar.

With the black dog at her side, they pressed on through the trees, avoiding the rabbit holes, ducking under some branches and climbing over others.

Ash stopped and held up the magic stone. 'It's beginning to glow,' she said. Ariel turned to see it. 'There must be something here,' she said. Ash nodded, then they carried on walking through the wood. Emitting a low growl, Archie stayed close to Ariel, his eyes fixed ahead.

In the middle of the Wild Wood, they stopped again. Ash held up her stone.

'Look at the hair on Archie's back,' said Ariel, noticing the dog's bristling coat.

Ash nodded, then coughed. 'Ergh, what's that horrible smell?' At the same time, the magic stone emitted a loud beep and a dull yellow light, and Archie gave a short, sharp bark, which made the sisters jump. Their hearts began to pump fast as they stared at the magic stone.

'We must be getting close,' said Ash.

Archie gave another sharp bark, followed by a deep growl. All the time his eyes were fixed on the back of the wood. Ariel grabbed his collar again and felt the dog strain forward as she held on. 'Archie, heel!' she said, trying to pull him back to her side.

Ash's eyes narrowed as she gazed slowly around the wood. 'I still can't see anything. Can you?'

'No,' said Ariel, biting her lip. 'But I can smell something horrible.'

'It's probably a dead rabbit.'

They stood for a moment, watching and waiting. Apart from Archie's growling, all was silent.

'This is creepy,' said Ariel. 'It feels as if the trees are getting closer.'

'Were these yellow eyes big enough for us to see in daylight?'

'I don't know.'

'Were they on the ground or in the trees?'

'They were in a bunch. I think they must have been on the ground.'

'I wonder what kind of creatures they are …' said Ash, thoughtfully. For a moment, they were silent, watchful. Then, clutching the stone in her hand, Ash stepped forward. 'Come on.'

They set off through the trees, Ariel holding onto Archie's collar and Ash holding onto the magic stone. Suddenly the stone gave another loud beep. Archie bounded forward and crashed through the trees. Thrown by the weight of the dog, Ariel fell to the ground. 'What is it?' she cried.

'I don't know!' said Ash, pulling her sister up. Their

hearts beat fast now. Close by, Archie barked at something on the ground in front of him.

'Blimey, that smell is *horrible!*' muttered Ariel, brushing off dead pine needles from her T-shirt.

'Come on,' said Ash. 'We've got to find out what Archie's barking at.'

Ariel gasped. 'I can't breathe with that smell.'

'Wait here, then.'

'No, I'm coming with you.'

'Archie, come here!' shouted Ash, but before she reached the dog, she stopped. She was now close to the far side of the Wild Wood and Archie was only two metres away. Still there were no yellow eyes to be seen. The smell was appalling – like putrefying flesh.

Suddenly, a terrible cold shudder ran through Ash's body. She gasped and grabbed a low branch. The magic stone in her other, closed, hand was pulsating hard. As Ariel reached her sister, she saw Ash's white face and wide eyes. Then she, too, shuddered. 'I feel like ice!' she cried.

As the two sisters clung to one another, Archie moved to stand in front of them, growling and barking. The hair on his back stood in a thick black ridge. His tail was high and his teeth bared.

'Look,' gasped Ash. She opened her hand to show

Ariel the magic stone. 'It's never been that colour before.'

Ariel stared at the sickly yellow light pulsating slowly in the stone. Another shudder ran through her body. 'Whatever they are, these things are not nice,' she whispered.

'But where *are* they?' said Ash, looking around. 'I can't see anything.'

Ariel shuddered. 'The smell … I'm going to be sick…' She turned away to vomit on the ground.

Ash took her little sister's arm and led her out of the Wild Wood. Archie stopped barking and followed at their side. Slowly and carefully, they picked their way back through the trees. When they reached the edge of the wood and walked into the sunlight, the girls flopped down onto the grass and drew in deep breaths of fresh air. Archie lay down beside them, panting.

Neither sister spoke for a while. Eventually, Ariel said, 'That was weird.'

'Totally bizarre,' agreed Ash.

'Whatever these eyes belong to, they're invisible in the daylight.'

'And what was that dreadful smell?' Ash rolled over and propped herself up on her elbow. 'My magic stone was warning us.' She held up the round, smooth stone in her hand. It glistened in the sunlight.

'I know.' Ariel pulled herself to sit cross-legged on the grass. 'Archie was going berserk.'

They were silent for a few seconds, then Ash said, 'Do you think we should tell Flame and Marina about the eyes?'

Ariel gave a hard laugh. 'You really think they'll want to know? They're too busy with their boyfriends to think about magic any more.'

Ash blinked and sat up. 'Is that what this is? I know it's strange, but does that make it magic?'

'It *felt* like magic,' said Ariel in a quiet voice.

Ash's face clouded. 'I hope it's not dark magic.'

Ariel sighed and rested her chin in her hands. 'Well it wasn't what I'd call "A Ball of Fun" magic with fairy godmothers and sparkly things.'

'But why now?' said Ash. 'And where's it coming from? Glenda's magic turned to good. Everything has been fine at Sprite Towers for nearly two years. Why would anybody else use magic here, now?'

'Everything in Sprite Towers is magic,' said Ariel. 'Sidney Sprite told me that and I know it deep inside me.'

Ash's face was thoughtful. 'So it attracts other magic, sometimes bad magic …'

'I wonder if it's something to do with that figure I saw behind the wall,' said Ariel. 'What was he or she doing there?'

'Mrs Duggery always told us there's no such thing as coincidence.'

Ariel nodded. 'Nothing happens by chance.' The sisters smiled: these phrases were favourite sayings amongst them.

'I wonder what Mrs Duggery would have advised us to do?' said Ash.

Ariel pursed her lips and thought for a moment. 'She would tell us to meet the threat, but to have all our wits about us.'

'And Grandma?'

'I think she would say the same.'

'I wonder when she'll be back from looking after her sick friend?'

Ariel shook her head. 'I'm not sure – but in that case, if we're to meet the threat and since we can't see the eyes in the daylight, I'll have to do another night flight. I know you don't want me to fly again, but how else will we know?'

Ash frowned. 'That's what I was thinking – or we could go into the Wild Wood once it's dark.'

Ariel snorted. 'No, thank you!'

'If you're going to do another flight, we'll have to camp out again. Are you sure you want to stay out here with these things about?'

Ariel's face was still pale. She thought for a while, then said, 'Archie will protect us.'

'But he may growl all night and we'd be terrified and we wouldn't sleep.'

The sisters were silent. Then Ash said, 'We could just forget about the eyes.'

'Do you think we should?'

'No – I don't think so. I was just wondering about that sickly yellow light.'

'You have a bad feeling?'

Ash nodded.

'I do, too,' said Ariel. 'But I think it's worth one more flight to find out if the eyes are still there.'

'All right, we'll camp out another night with Archie and you do a short flight. Agreed?'

Ariel nodded. 'Agreed.'

Ash drew herself up. 'Now it's time to cook some Cheese Toasties on the campfire. I'm hungry. How are you feeling?'

'Ravenous,' said Ariel, getting up, and for the next hour they were busy with the campfire and the business of eating.

That night, when everything was still, Ash used some gentle binding magic on Archie, so that he would not start barking when they left him in the caravan. When he was settled, the sisters crept out of the door and walked over the lawn. In the shadow of a big oak tree, hidden from the house, Ariel lifted off and flew up into the sky. Ash watched her with some degree of envy. I'd love to do that, she thought, as she saw her sister soar through the air.

It did not take Ariel long to fly over the Wild Wood and see the yellow eyes looking up at her. As soon as she saw them, she felt the same sense of fear she had felt the night before. Then she caught the briefest glimpse of a figure standing in the trees. Quickly, she flew down and landed on the grass behind the oak tree where Ash was waiting.

In the moonlight, Ash noted her sister's white face. 'Are they still there?'

'They've moved forward to the centre of the Wild Wood.'

'Did you see anyone?'

'Yes – I think so. In the trees.'

Ash gulped. 'What, inside the wall?'

Ariel nodded, panting to catch her breath.

'But that's not far from the caravan!'

The two girls stared at one another. A brown owl screeched and they jumped. Suddenly the night felt very cold.

'I'm frightened,' whispered Ariel.

'So am I.' Ash looked around her. 'Should we go back to the house?'

'Mum and Dad will want to know what's happened.'

'Perhaps we should tell them,' said Ash. 'Dad would go and have a look in the Wild Wood.'

'But if those yellow eyes are magic, it would be better to deal with it ourselves,' said Ariel.

'But what about the figure in the wood?'

For a moment they hesitated, then Ariel whispered, 'Archie will protect us.' Then as fast as they could, they ran to the caravan and locked the door behind them.

Chapter Six
Tuesday
MAGIC REVEALED

For the rest of the night the girls slept fitfully, their dreams strange and unsettling. When Archie needed to go out next morning, he woke Ash by licking her hand. She got up and opened the caravan door, then, yawning, crawled back into her sleeping bag. By mid-morning Ottalie was worried that she had not seen her daughters, so went down to the caravan and found them sound asleep.

Ash and Ariel got up and went up to the house for a shower. Over a late breakfast, Ottalie commented that they seemed to be in a daze, which the girls explained away as having talked half the night. When Flame and Marina appeared, there was little communication. Both older girls had their noses pressed to their mobiles, busy responding to a stream of calls and texts. Marina was friendly, when otherwise unengaged, but Flame took almost no notice of her younger sisters.

'See,' whispered Ariel, pointedly, to Ash. 'They won't want to help us.'

Ash smiled, but said nothing. Of the four sisters,

she had the calmest character and was the only one who didn't flounce. Ash's innate sense of balance enabled her to detach and see the overall view. Flame had a quick temper and was easily irritated. She told people straightaway if she didn't like something they were doing. Marina liked everyone to be happy, so she went with the flow as much as possible but often got upset. Like Flame, Ariel was easily piqued and the two often clashed these days. This was partly because Ariel refused to be put down just because she was the youngest. It was also because Flame had always been protective of her little sister, but no longer played this role and this annoyed Ariel. Munching her muesli at the kitchen table, Ariel reasoned that she could do with some protection when the Wild Wood was full of things that watched her at night but became invisible by day, drove the dog wild and gave off the most terrible smell. She glowered at Flame, but her eldest sister took no notice. Flame was busy organising another game of tennis.

'If you get any closer to your mobile, your nose will get stuck to it permanently,' muttered Ariel. Flame ignored her. Ariel stabbed her spoon into the bowl.

'Quinn and Zak will be here at two o'clock,' Flame said to Marina, across the table.

Marina smiled. 'Okay,' she said, then looked down, feeling shy, suddenly, aware that everyone was watching her. Yes, she did like Zak, but she didn't want to make a fool of herself over this boy. She thought about how little she knew about him. Unlike her and her sisters, Zak talked little about his family. He had told her that they had recently moved to the town as his father was starting a new business in the county. His father knew Quinn's father, so the boys had been introduced. Zak would be attending Drysdale's in the autumn with Quinn and the Sprite Sisters. Zak looked dreamy, to be sure, but Marina had noted a strange expression on his face at times and it unnerved her. She had the sense that he could see into her mind. At these times his eyes reminded her of a hawk, all-seeing. She was dazzled by him, but she would be careful.

Ash and Ariel ate their breakfast, each wondering about the yellow eyes and if they should tell their sisters. Now did not seem like a good time. A few minutes later, they cleared up and went their different ways. Ottalie took Ariel to the dentist. Flame and Marina went back to their rooms. Ash went down to the stables to feed and water the rabbits and guinea pigs. Seeing after the animals was another thing that Flame and Marina no longer took much part in. The younger girls were fond of their pets, however, so it was an enjoyable task. Ash put the guinea pigs out in a long wire run on the lawn and sat down to watch them nibbling the grass.

It was then that her fingers started to tingle. She stared down at her hands, then flexed and wiggled her fingers. Was it pins and needles? No, they were definitely tingling. The image of Ariel soaring through the night sky flashed through her mind. How she would love to fly in the air like that!

In her pocket, the magic stone beeped. She pulled it out and held it in the palm of her hand. It glowed a beautiful bright blue. At that moment Ash knew, with an absolute certainty, that her magic power was calling her. The tingling in her fingers was her power of Earth waking up. It was alive and needed to be used. The magic stone was glowing blue to make sure she took note.

As she sat on the grass, Ash was conscious that Grandma had always been firm that the sisters should not play with their power. Magic power, Grandma said, was only to be used for good. But now there were strange things in the Wild Wood, and if her magic was needed – and why else would her fingers tingle and the stone light up? – she wouldn't be 'playing'. Ever careful and steady in her thinking, Ash considered the responsibility of having a magic power. For a few minutes, she looked at the stone's glowing light and felt the tingling in her fingers. Then, with a sense of resolve, she made up her mind. She would practise her power of Earth.

Where Ariel had the power to lift things – and now herself – with her power of Air, Ash's power was to bind. When she pointed her finger to use her power, she could fix something or someone to the spot as if they had grown roots. As she got up from the grass and walked to the camp, she wondered what would happen if she used her magic on the shadowy figure in the woods. She might fix them to the spot, but what then? Alone, in the dark, it would be unwise to confront the intruder.

As Ash reached the camp, her fingers were tingling so much that it was beginning to feel uncomfortable. What could she bind, she wondered, looking around. Would her power be stronger now, as Ariel said hers was? And, if so, would her power work over a greater distance?

Her eyes fixed on a pair of pigeons flapping about on a branch high in an oak tree some distance away. It was a mock fight, a struggle for territory. Ash pointed her right index finger at one of the pigeons and summoned her power. Whoosh, she felt it course through her hand and come out of her finger in a huge wave – and the pigeon was fixed, for the moment, to the branch. She pointed her finger at the second pigeon – and whoosh, out flowed her power and bound the bird to the branch. Both pigeons were immobilised.

Ash held up her right hand and gazed at her finger.

Instinctively, she knew that her power had changed: it would never have worked at such a distance before. It has grown stronger, she thought, and she pointed her finger at each of the pigeons and released them from the branch. Immediately they started fighting again.

Could I use my power to bind myself to the ground? If Ariel can use her power of Air to fly, surely I could use my power of Earth to grow roots … Maybe I could burrow into the earth like a mole or pull down a cloud from the sky …

Then Ash remembered another aspect of her power of Earth, which was to be able to put her hands on something and sense what was behind it. Sitting down on the ground, she laid her hands, palms down, on the grass. She closed her eyes and asked her power of Earth to show her what was beneath her hands. Images of soil, worms, larvae, stones, bones and grit flashed through her mind, followed by chalk, water, then more chalk and more water, then rock. Down and down her mind went through the earth's crust, then the mantle. Hotter and hotter her hands felt, until she saw in her mind bright orange, the molten core of the planet and her hands were sizzling.

Ash lifted up her hands and stared at them. That was amazing, she thought. And she did the same thing again. This time, however, she slowed down her mind, so that she could take in the images as they flashed by. This time she noticed something she had not seen before: the creatures that live in the molten crevices, deep in the earth. This time she saw them: insect-like 'things' that crawl through the fissures, inured to the heat by millions of years of existence.

Ash shuddered, revolted by this image of the insects, and pulled her mind back closer to the surface of the earth, then up and back. She was sitting there staring at her hands when Ariel ran into the camp.

'There you are!'

Ash smiled as Ariel flopped down beside her on the grass. 'You've been practising,' said Ariel.

Ash nodded.

'And?'

'And I found I could "see" what was beneath the ground, right to the centre of the earth.'

Ariel's eyes grew wide. 'That's nearly four thousand miles! Wow! And?'

'And there are horrible insects that crawl around under the crust.'

'Errgh.'

'The heat was incredible.'

They were silent for a moment, then Ariel said, 'Why don't the insects melt if it's that hot?'

Ash shook her head. 'I believe there are some

insects that are virtually indestructible – cockroaches, for instance. Anyway, that's what I felt in my hands and saw in my mind.'

Ariel squirmed. 'I hate things that crawl.' She thought about this for a moment then asked, 'Do you think the things with yellow eyes crawl?'

Ash considered this. 'You said they'd moved forward and that they're on the ground, so they probably crawl.'

Ariel held up her hands and wiggled her fingers as if they were creepy-crawlies. 'Moving through the Wild Wood, creeping towards Sprite Towers ….'

'We don't know that,' said Ash.

'Oh for heaven's sakes, Ash!' said Ariel, dropping her hands to her sides.

'Well, we don't!'

'What are we going to do?'

Ash frowned. 'I don't know.'

'I'm not camping out again.'

'Nor me.'

Ariel sighed. 'I wish Mrs Duggery were here. She had such powerful magic and would have known what to do.'

'We all miss her,' said Ash.

Ariel rested her chin on her hands and gave another sigh.

'The yellow-eyed things might go away,' said Ash.

Ariel snorted. 'You always look on the bright side.'

Ash laughed. 'Well, let's wait and see. But you're not to fly again – please.'

'How will we know if the eyes are getting closer?'

'We'll see from the top of the house if they leave the Wild Wood.'

Ariel shuddered.

Ash turned. 'Quinn and Zak are here – I hear sounds of laughter from the tennis court.'

Despite Ash's calm approach to the eyes in the Wild Wood, she felt unsettled inside. Ariel's impression of creepy-crawlies stayed in the back of her mind, until she and Ariel started to build a course for a bicycle race on the lawn. The circuit involved cycling up and down various ramps, around poles and boxes, under a rope stretched between two trees, then picking up potatoes from buckets without falling off. With much hilarity, the two girls added more and more elements to the course and by the time that Flame and Marina and the two boys finished their game of tennis there was so much noise they all came to investigate.

Quinn and Zak immediately borrowed the girls' bicycles and began to race one another with much bravado. Flame and Marina ran to get their bicycles from the shed and joined in. More bicycles were found and soon all six of them were cycling furiously round the course in the sweltering August heat. Everybody was shouting and laughing and Archie was running in circles.

When Ottalie laid the table for tea under the big copper beech tree at the side of the lawn, they were all ready for a rest. As she smoothed the checked blue and white tablecloth across the table, Zak got off his bicycle and ran to offer to help. Ottalie noted his good manners and quick thinking. A minute later, he and Marina went to the kitchen, then carried back trays of homemade cakes and jugs of cold lemonade.

In the kitchen Flame made a big pot of tea and assembled cups and saucers, while outside Quinn brought chairs around the table. Ariel ran to get Archie a bowl of water and Ash carried down a plate of scones, stuffed with cream and jam. Quinn helped Flame with the tea tray. A minute later, they all sat down in the shade of the tree and tucked in. Flame poured the tea. Marina poured cold lemonade into tall glasses. Ottalie handed out the scones and cut her freshly-made fruitcake into slices.

A short while later, Colin Sprite joined them. Embarrassed by her parents these days, Flame winced at her father's easy manner and good humour. But as Quinn and Zak clearly enjoyed it, she relaxed and the conversation flowed.

Of them all, perhaps Ariel enjoyed the experience of sitting there the most. For the first time in months she felt the closeness of her older sisters. For once none of the girls was bickering. Everyone was chattering and laughing. It was as it used to be, thought Ariel, looking around.

As the tea drew to a close, Ariel noticed that her father was talking to Zak. Sitting next to him, Marina was gazing slyly at the boy. Ariel wondered if her father could feel Zak's hawk-like eyes looking into his mind. And as she wondered this, her father turned away to talk to Flame and Zak turned his head to look across at her. Ariel felt as if Zak had caught her thought. His eyes were so penetrating, his gaze so direct that she drew a sharp breath. It was if he was saying, 'I know what you are thinking.'

Zak's gaze was for a brief moment, but as he turned away to speak to Marina, his eyes caught the light. It was for a split second only, but Ariel saw it – and she blinked in astonishment. No, no, she thought. It can't be! Zak looked back at Ariel with a mysterious smile – and she knew that what she had seen was true, and that he wanted her to know it.

Ariel shuddered. She had the sudden feeling that something was crawling up her back. She looked round at Ash, who looked at her with concern. 'What?' her face seemed to say.

'The light – the light in Zak's eyes,' Ariel wanted to tell her.

The light was yellow.

Chapter Seven
TRUTHS SPOKEN

That night, as the moon was high in the sky, Ariel and Ash crept out of their bedrooms and up the staircase to the attics on the third floor. At the top, they stopped and listened. All was quiet.

Ash turned on her torch and led the way along the corridor to one of the attic rooms that faced south over the lawn. Fumbling in the darkness, Ariel tripped on the rough wooden floorboards.

'Sssh,' whispered Ash, helping her up. 'We don't want to wake Mum.'

Ariel winced as she rubbed her ankle. Holding up her torch, Ash asked, 'Are you okay?'

Ariel nodded and they crept towards the window.

Ash shivered. 'It's cold up here.'

Ariel didn't notice the temperature. As she peered out of the casement window, her eyes were focused on the edge of the Wild Wood. 'Look there,' she whispered, pointing at the long line of yellow eyes that were fixed on Sprite Towers.

Ash started. 'Crikey, I didn't realise the eyes would be so big! Whatever could they be?'

Ariel shook her head. 'I don't know.'

'How could we not have seen these creatures in the Wild Wood?'

They were silent as they stared down. Then Ash whispered, 'What should we do?'

Ariel shook her head. 'I don't know. The things have moved forward and will soon be on the lawn if they keep going.'

'You said you saw a yellow light in Zak's eyes this afternoon.'

Ariel nodded. 'I think he wanted me to see it.'

'Why do you think that?'

'There was something in his expression – sort of "Look at me". He held my gaze and I had the feeling he intended me to see the yellow light in his eyes.'

They were silent for a moment, then Ash whispered, 'Do you think that he may be down there?'

'I can't see anyone in the trees, but I wouldn't expect to from up here at night.'

Staring down into the darkness, Ash's heart began to pound. 'We must tell Flame and Marina.'

'They'll never believe Zak is involved.'

'We don't know that he is, for sure.'

'Yes, we do.'

'No, we *don't* Ariel!'

'How else would you explain his eyes going yellow then?'

Ash shook her head, 'I don't know.'

Ariel whispered, 'Whether Zak is involved or not, we need to stop the yellow-eyed things getting to the house.'

'That I agree on,' said Ash. 'And I think we should tell Flame and Marina that someone is creeping about outside.'

'But not that it may be Zak.'

'Exactly.'

The two sisters crept back across the floorboards and down the staircase to the second floor. Marina was surprised to be woken in the middle of the night, but registered the frightened look in her sisters' eyes. She got up, pulled on her dressing gown and slippers and crept along the corridor. Flame woke quickly, but was less than enthusiastic to be dragged out of bed. With some degree of irritability, she followed her sisters up to the attics.

Ash led the way with the torch as the four Sprite Sisters tiptoed across the floorboards of the attic room. Then they huddled up against the window and peered down.

'So what have I been dragged up here to look at?' muttered Flame, shivering.

'Look towards the edge of the Wild Wood,' whispered Ash.

Marina pushed back her dark curly hair and peered out of the dusty window. Suddenly she gasped, 'What are all those yellow eyes?'

Flame leaned forward, ducking a cobweb. 'Where?'

'There – look, along the edge of the lawn. Can you see?'

Flame peered out of the window. Suddenly she started. 'There's a lot of yellow eyes staring at the house.'

'I know,' whispered Ariel.

'What *are* they?' asked Flame.

'We don't know,' said Ash. 'They appeared right at the back of the Wild Wood, by the wall, a few days ago and they've been moving forward since.'

'Whatever they are, they give off the most terrible smell,' whispered Ariel.

'You've seen them?' said Flame.

'No – that's it,' said Ash. 'When we searched the Wild Wood in the daylight, we couldn't *see* anything.'

'But we could smell something,' said Ariel. 'The pong was vile. It made me sick.'

'Sssh, everybody, too loud,' said Marina, in a soft voice.

'And Archie went bonkers,' whispered Ash, very softly. 'He growled and barked at something.'

'He seemed to be able to see the things but we couldn't,' added Ariel.

'So you can only see the eyes at night?' whispered Flame.

Ash and Ariel nodded. Huddled together, the four sisters stared out of the window.

'Why are they here? What do they want?' whispered Marina.

'I don't know, but their gaze doesn't waver,' whispered Ash. 'They're all staring at Sprite Towers.'

Marina shuddered.

As she stared into the darkness, Flame Sprite tightened her mouth, felt her heartbeat quicken. Something that had been put to the back of her mind for a long while suddenly jumped forward – and she was not comfortable. Her magic power, she had thought, had been stowed away. It was a thing of the past. This had suited Flame: her life now was centred on Quinn and her friends. She couldn't think about magic power and have a boyfriend who she couldn't tell, she had reasoned. Now, as she looked down, she had the sense that the yellow eyes staring back would call upon the part of her that she had tried to forget. Gazing into the dark, Flame had the sense that Sprite Towers might need to be protected.

Something else stirred in Flame's mind: why were

these things here now? What had happened to call them here? Her intuition suddenly alert, she turned to Ash and Ariel and whispered, 'Have either of you been using your magic powers?'

Ash gasped in surprise. 'Why do you ask that?'

'Nothing happens by chance and I just wondered,' whispered Flame. 'The last time we got "invaded" was on your ninth birthday, Ariel, the day you came into your power. That was also the day Glenda Glass moved to the village. Well – have you, Ariel?'

Ariel glared silently out of the window.

'Don't blame Ariel,' said Ash.

'Okay, but I still want to know if she has.'

Ariel remained silent. Pressed up together by the window, the sisters felt the tension increase between them and they started to move apart. Marina said softly, 'Can we talk about this in my room, so we can get warm? It's freezing up here.'

They crept back down the stairs and into Marina's bedroom. She turned on her bedside lamp, then climbed under the duvet with Ash and Ariel. Wrapped in her dressing gown, Flame sat down on the chair at the side of the bed and whispered to Ariel. 'Tell me what's been going on.'

Ariel's expression hardened as she looked at Flame. 'You look like a headmistress. Always bossing us about.'

'Sssh, you two or we'll wake Mum,' hissed Marina. She looked at Flame. 'Why do you think something's been going on?'

Flame made a face as if to say, 'Come on'. Marina sighed, aware that once Flame got started on something it was difficult to stop her.

'Flame, please don't start – it's too late at night to argue,' said Ash, holding out her hand. 'Let Ariel explain.'

Ariel started by telling them about her desire to fly – to which Flame reacted with horror. In angry whispers, the eldest and the youngest Sprite Sister argued about experimenting with their magic power and what would happen if their mother found out, until Marina told Flame to shut up. 'For heaven's sake, let Ariel explain!' she said.

Flame sat back in her chair and crossed her long arms over her chest. Ash then told them she how had seen Ariel soar through the night sky and how she had felt envious of her little sister's power.

Marina smiled at Ariel with pride. 'Did you really fly over the house?' she whispered. Ariel nodded, grinning, and they huddled closer.

Flare glared at her and muttered, 'I knew it.' Ariel glared back. Then, in a soft voice, Ash explained how

Ariel's flight had allowed her to see the yellow eyes and they should be grateful.

'And I saw a figure in the woods,' added Ariel.

Flame and Marina looked at one another with alarm.

'When?' said Flame, turning to Ariel.

'Saturday night and Monday night.'

Flame's frown was turning to anger. 'How many times have you flown, Ariel?

Ariel crossed her arms and put her nose in the air. 'Four times.'

'I watched Ariel on the fourth go,' said Ash. 'She was checking if the eyes were still there.'

'Did you ever stop to think what Grandma will say about this?' said Flame.

'Please could we talk about that later, Flame,' said Marina. 'Ariel, who was it you saw?'

'I don't know who it was,' said Ariel. 'I could only see a tall, shadowy figure.'

Flame blew out hard. 'Well, this complicates things.'

'Yes,' said Marina.

'Are the figure and the yellow eyes connected, I wonder?' said Flame.

They fell silent. Flame unfolded her arms and sat forward in the chair – her mind now engaged, her thoughts moving from Ariel's experiment to the bigger problem of the intruder and the yellow eyes. Marina, Ash and Ariel watched as she got up from her chair and tiptoed to the window. Pulling back the curtains, Flame looked out. From this first floor window she could not see the edge of the Wild Wood as the ground sloped away, but she had a clear view of the lawn to the back of the house.

As she stared into the darkness, Flame drew in a sharp breath and motioned to her sisters to come and look. 'Sssh,' she whispered, aware that their parents were one floor below. Marina, Ash and Ariel tiptoed over the carpet and crowded round the window.

The Sprite Sisters gasped in horror. The yellow eyes had moved forward and were now at the edge of the lawn.

'What are we going to do?' whispered Ash, with a look of alarm. They all looked at Flame – and waited. Flame's face was tense with confusion. Should she use her magic power again? Is this who she still was, despite growing older? What would her mother say, if she found out? How would she keep her magic power secret from Quinn? These thoughts rushed round her brain. Flame Sprite, usually so decisive, was perplexed.

Ariel broke the silence. 'Well, I'm going down.' She turned from the window and started to move quietly towards the door.

'Ariel, stop!' whispered Marina.

'Ariel, wait!' whispered Ash. Ariel turned and looked back. 'Just hang on a mo, please,' said Ash.

Flame turned from the window and looked across the room at Ariel, registered her little sister's angry face.

'Don't you want to protect Sprite Towers?' hissed Ariel.

Flame's face blazed. 'Yes, of course I do! You don't understand – that's not the point!'

'What *is* the point?' said Ariel, in an angry whisper.

'Sssh, for goodness sakes, or we'll all get caught,' said Marina.

Ash looked from one sister to the other.

'Well?' whispered Ariel.

For a moment everybody waited, then Flame said, 'It's not the same for me now. I'm older. I don't want my magic to start up again. I don't want to have to keep things secret from Quinn.'

Marina nodded. 'I understand that. I feel the same with my friends.'

Ariel shrugged. 'Well, I don't.'

Ash said quietly, 'Flame, I'm not sure you have a choice right now.'

Flame gave a long sigh and nodded. 'Okay then.'

'We'd better put some clothes on,' whispered Marina.

Five minutes later they crept down the staircase, through the hallway and into the kitchen. As Archie woke in his basket, Ash put a gentle binding spell on him to stop him growling and barking: the last thing they wanted now was for Mum and Dad to be disturbed.

Then, as quietly as they could, the Sprite Sisters opened the back door and stepped out into the night.

Chapter Eight
WONKY MAGIC

It was just after two o'clock when the Sprite Sisters walked over the lawn. The moon was barely visible behind the clouds, the night dark and damp. The girls walked apart, but drew closer as they got nearer to the row of yellow eyes. By the time they stopped, around ten metres away from the eyes, they were standing side by side, their hearts racing and their faces white.

Flame stood alert, scanned the line of eyes, noticed their unblinking stare. Whatever they were, the things appeared to be on the ground. Their eyes were big enough and bright enough to be seen from the house but, paradoxically, small enough to remain unseen in the daylight. How could the creatures be invisible in the daylight? If they vanished, where did they go? For a few seconds, she tried to work out the size of the eyes; from where she was standing, Flame concluded each eye looked the size of a mug.

'This is so weird,' whispered Marina.

Flame held her ear to one side. 'What's that sound?'

'What, the clicking?' whispered Ash.

'It sounds like knitting needles,' said Marina.

'Or insects,' said Flame. 'You know that noise when you get a swarm? They sound a bit like that.'

Marina shuddered. 'Insects? Do you think these things are some kind of insect?'

Flame stared at the yellow eyes. 'I don't know what we're dealing with, but I don't think they're nice.'

'They look malevolent,' whispered Ash.

'Well, they're giving me the creeps,' said Marina.

In the darkness, the yellow-eyed things edged forward again. Flame took a deep breath. 'They can see us standing here, but it's not stopping them.'

'Will they hurt us?' said Ariel.

'I don't know,' said Flame.

'What the heck *are* they?' whispered Ariel. Then she put her hand over her nose and spluttered. 'Ugh, that smell ...'

Flame scanned the trees and lawn. 'Can anyone see the figure?'

Ariel and Marina looked round. 'No,' they said.

Ash's attention was now focused on her magic stone, which lay in her open palm. It pulsated slowly, emanating a sickly yellow light. 'See this,' she whispered. Her sisters turned to look, their faces tense, their eyes wide.

'I've never seen it go that colour before,' said Marina.

'I think the stone is telling us these things have evil magic,' whispered Ash.

Their hearts pumping fast now, the Sprite Sisters moved closer together.

'The eyes are definitely getting nearer,' whispered Marina.

Ariel moved back a few steps to catch her breath, her hand still over her nose.

Ash pushed her magic stone into her pocket and turned to Flame. 'What shall we do?'

Flame hesitated as her mother's face, then Quinn's face, flashed through her mind. How would she keep this secret? 'We promised Mum we wouldn't use our magic power again,' she whispered.

Ash said, 'I know, Flame, but we've got to try to stop these creatures coming closer. They might try to get into the house.'

'We could try running at them and shooing them away,' said Flame, but as she said it, she knew this would never work. Ash was right: there was malevolence here.

Flame and Ash looked at one another. 'We must protect Sprite Towers,' said Ash.

'And ourselves,' whispered Marina.

Ariel said, 'She's right, Flame.'

'But we promised,' said Flame.

They waited. Flame frowned and bit her bottom lip,

part of her still uncertain. It wasn't just Mum or Quinn; suddenly, she felt thirteen again. Images of the battles the Sprite Sisters had fought with Glenda Glass, and the magic power they had used the year before last, flickered through her mind. She'd thought she'd finished with magic, but here she was, fifteen years old and with a boyfriend, standing on the lawn with her sisters, about to use her power of Fire. Their Sprite cousin Verena, who had magic power, would understand, but what would her friends say if they found out? Would she ever fit in?

'Flame?' whispered Marina.

This is no time to stand and think, thought Flame. It's time to act. She looked round at Ash. 'Can you bind down the things?'

Ash nodded and moved a little apart. Facing the line of yellow eyes, she lifted her hands and pointed her index fingers. Summoning her power of Earth, she sent out a huge bolt of magic. As it flashed from Ash's hands, the yellow eyes drooped, then closed, and the clicking noise stopped. For a moment all was dark and still. The Sprite Sisters held their breath and waited. Then, one by one, the yellow eyes opened and stared back at them. Incredulous, the sisters looked at one another.

 Ash stared at her hands. Her power had felt so strong – stronger than it had ever been – but it had not bound the things to the ground. The yellow eyes crept a little closer over the damp grass. Flame and Marina glanced at Ash, wondering if her power really had become stronger. It had certainly seemed so to them.

'I'll try,' said Ariel, moving forwards. With all her might, she sent out the strongest wind she could muster. Her sisters watched in awe as the strength of her magic sent a narrow tunnel of wind blasting over the grass. As it hit the yellow-eyed things, they wobbled and fell sideways, but remained on the ground. The girls waited as the wind subsided. A few seconds later, the yellow eyes lifted and stared back at them. Ariel gasped in surprise. 'This is unreal.'

The clicking sound was getting louder and the smell of decaying flesh was so strong that the girls began to gasp for breath. Aware that it had been a long while since she had practised her magic power of Water, Marina held up her hands. Taking a deep breath, she conjured up a wave of water to wash away the things. Magic power – stronger than it had ever been before – coursed through her fingers. To the right of the line of yellow eyes, a huge wave appeared on the lawn, but Marina panicked and lost control of her power. As the wave of water passed over the yellow eyes, it changed direction and surged towards the girls. They ran back, only just missing it, and when they looked around the eyes were still there, watching them. With their hearts pounding hard, the

Sprite Sisters looked at one another in complete disbelief. Why wasn't their magic having any effect?

Flame walked forward, stood tall and strong. With her arms and hands flexed, all doubts about using her power were dispelled by the threat now facing her. She held out her hands and blasted the yellow-eyed things with her power of Fire, but the scorching flame that seared over them had no effect. Still the eyes stared back. Flame stared at her fingers, realising that she had only just been able to control her power. It had become much stronger, she thought – but it had not worked.

None of the sisters' magic powers had been strong enough to stop the line of yellow-eyes. In the darkness, foul air enveloped the sisters.

Suddenly, Ariel said, 'Quick – we need to make the Circle of Power!'

The girls ran back towards the house and formed a circle holding hands. Panting with fear, they tried to clear their minds to create the magic blue light that had protected them in the past. Tightly they gripped each other's hands as they summoned the circle of light that would engulf and protect them.

'Focus,' said Marina, biting her lip.

'Come on …' muttered Ash.

'Where's it gone?' said Flame.

For a brief moment the blue light appeared, but

instead of the feeling of calm that usually came when they made the Circle of Power, the sisters felt their magic jangling against each other. Their powers were too erratic and scattered to hold the circle and the light subsided.

Ariel broke the circle. 'It's not working!' she cried, turning away. 'We're not in tune like we used to be. Everything has changed …'

Flame, Marina and Ash let go of each other's hands and looked at one another with worried eyes. Ariel was right. Each of them had felt her magic power, but the light that had protected them before was now elusive. They looked round at the line of yellow eyes with a sense of hopelessness.

'I'm so tired,' said Marina.

'There's nothing we can do now,' said Flame.

Ash put her arm around Ariel's shoulder and they walked back to the house. When they reached the back door, they all took off their trainers. As they crept through the kitchen, Ash removed the binding spell she had put on Archie. They climbed the stairs, weary and worried. They had failed to stop the yellow-eyed creatures. They had failed to create the Circle of Power.

As the evil magic moved closer, the Sprite Sisters fell into uneasy sleep.

Chapter Nine
Wednesday
DOUBTS

Flame stared up at the ceiling. She had slept fitfully and woken early, unsettled by the events of last night. Using her magic power had been exciting – she had forgotten how much she had missed it – but with it had come a feeling of unease. It reminded her how close she used to feel to her sisters and of the adventures they had shared, but it showed how much she had changed and how things had changed between them.

Flame was aware that her magic power bound her to her sisters, but set her apart from her friends. Here she was, half girl, half young woman, unsure of herself in a way she had never been. In another hour or so, her mobile phone would start beeping messages from her friends and the chattering would resume. Flame did not want to feel different. She wanted to fit in, but as a Sprite with magic power she would never completely do so. She might look the same, but she would always be different – from everyone her own age, except her sisters and Verena. If her cousin had been here now, they would be talking about the dilemma of having a magic power and being 'different'. But Verena was on holiday with her parents and Flame felt this was not something she could text about. Magic power was secret and could only be spoken about face to face.

Verena's family had been away all summer, but she would see her cousin soon when they started school. From the autumn, Flame and Marina would be boarding with Verena at Drysdale's. Flame and Marina were so involved with music, drama and sport at the school that they got home late in the evenings. Ottalie and Colin had decided it would be easier for them all if the older girls boarded during the week.

Flame smiled to herself. It's funny how things change, she thought. She used to loathe Verena. The two girls were fiercely competitive at school, matched academically and in sport. Flame had disliked Verena's cold, disdainful manner. It was not difficult to annoy Flame, but Verena could do it in seconds. But, as Marina made friends with Verena and began to understand her and talk about her, Flame began to realise the girl's coldness was a mask to hide her loneliness.

Flame thought back to when Verena's grandmother, Glenda Glass, moved to The Oaks, two summers ago. Close to Sprite Towers, the house belonged to Verena's father, Stephen. When Verena's mother, Zoe, ran away (or so they all thought at the time), Stephen asked his mother to come and look after Verena. Glenda moved in and, almost immediately, used her dark magic against the Sprite Sisters. For the next six months, it seemed to be one battle after another, as Glenda tried to hurt the sisters and get Sprite Towers. The Sprite Sisters used their powers of Fire, Water, Earth and Air to protect themselves and the house. Providing the four sisters used their magic power together, they could defeat Glenda's dark magic.

As time went on and the battles with Glenda continued, Flame began to wonder if Verena had inherited the magic power that ran through the Sprite family. Since Verena was living with her grandmother, Flame began to worry that the girl could be influenced by Glenda's dark power. Then, Verena found her own magic power and she told the Sprite Sisters. At the same time, Flame found a map that led them to the 'treasure' that Mrs Duggery had told them was hidden at Sprite Towers in something she called the Crossed Circle.

It transpired that this treasure was not material: it was a way to restore the balance in the family and to bring harmony. Verena was a key part of this magic – and so was Glenda. Prompted by her granddaughter's angry reaction to the pain she had caused, Glenda began to have doubts about the effects of her dark magic. She realised it was not bringing her any happiness. When

Verena asked her to help them create the Crossed Circle, Glenda had agreed, albeit reluctantly.

And they had created such magic that day! There had been eight Sprites: Flame and her sisters, Verena, Violet Duggery, Glenda Glass and Marilyn, her grandmother. After losing her magic power many years ago, Marilyn had found it was restored that day. Together, they stood in a circle in the West Tower and used their magic power to create the rainbow of light that would create the Crossed Circle. And it worked, remembered Flame. In front of them, a panorama of ghostly Sprites walked around within the Crossed Circle: Sprites who had passed away many years before. The sisters had seen their great-great-grandfather Sidney and his wife, Mim, clear as day. Balance was restored in the whole Sprite family, past, present and future. Since then, the family had been at peace.

But still the secret must be kept about the magic power of the Sprite family, thought Flame. She moved up the bed and propped herself up on her right elbow. A beam of sunlight streamed through the gap in her curtains. As she watched it flicker on the carpet, she remembered how the power of Fire first coursed through her fingers on her ninth birthday. Since then, she had kept the Sprite family secret. I can't talk about my magic, even to my closest friends, she thought. If they knew, they'd probably think I was some kind of freak …

This was not just about fitting in, she thought, with a frown. A threat was approaching Sprite Towers and the sisters' magic had not halted it. They had failed to stop the yellow-eyed things.

Thoughts whirred in Flame's mind. I used my magic power for the first time in a long while last night – and it had no effect. Has my power changed? Are these things more malevolent than we realise? What are they? What do they want? How do we stop them? Who is the figure in the woods?

And so on. After a while, exhausted, Flame lay back against the pillow and fell into an uneasy sleep. She dreamed that things were crawling all over her and she saw Zak's face smiling a strange smile. By the time she woke and went down for breakfast, she was tired, irritable and in a thoroughly bad mood.

One by one, the Sprite Sisters appeared at the breakfast table.

'Whatever is the matter with you all this morning?' said Ottalie, looking round at them. Nobody answered and thankfully the telephone rang. While Ottalie was speaking, their father came in from outside with a puzzled look on his face. 'There's a big scorch mark on the lawn,' he said. Nobody replied.

'Was there lightning last night?' said Colin, as he

sat down at the table. The Sprite Sisters shook their heads and concentrated on eating their breakfast.

'Oh well, the grass will soon grow again,' said Colin, pouring a cup of coffee. Flame tried to look as non-plussed as possible, but she suddenly gave a huge yawn. Colin blinked in surprise. Quickly Flame put her hand over her mouth and mumbled, 'Sorry'.

Marina buttered a piece of toast. Ariel stared at the table as she ate her scrambled egg. Ash drank her apple juice and smiled wanly at her father. Flame's phone beeped and she picked it up and blearily read the text message. Then Marina's mobile beeped.

Colin frowned. 'Here we go again – noses to the mobiles. Whatever happened to conversation?'

Ariel giggled. 'It's the "new" conversation, Dad.'

He gave her a sad smile. 'You'll be the same in another year or so.'

'Not me,' said Ariel. 'I can't stand mobiles.'

'How will you communicate with your friends then?'

'I will talk to them face to face,' said Ariel.

Colin gave a short laugh. 'Good luck, love,' he said. He looked round the table. 'Your mother is right: you all look exhausted this morning. Whatever is the matter?'

'Bad night, Dad,' said Ash, with another wan smile.

'Me too,' said Ariel. Flame and Marina were so

absorbed in their texting they had not heard. As soon as Flame put her phone down it beeped again. Colin raised his eyebrows and said sharply, 'Hells bells, girls, no texting at the table, please.'

With sulky faces, Flame and Marina turned off their phones. When Ottalie came back into the kitchen, everybody was eating in silence. She threw Flame and Marina an exasperated look and sat down. 'Teenagers,' she said to her husband.

Colin nodded. 'Permanently exhausted and surgically attached to their mobiles, it seems. With any luck, they might start talking to us again in a few years. What do you think?'

Ottalie gave a big sigh. 'I hope so.' At the same time, all four sisters yawned. Their parents stared at them in astonishment. Mumbling apologies, the girls got up from the table, cleared their plates and left the kitchen. Immediately, Flame and Marina turned on their phones.

'My room,' snapped Flame, as they climbed the stairs. As they reached her room, Flame walked in and flopped down on her bed. Marina wandered in, reading a text. Hesitant and awkward, Ash and Ariel stood in the doorway. It was clear their older sister was in a foul mood and, anyway, her bedroom was normally off-limits these days.

'For heaven's sake, come in and sit down,' said

Flame. Ash and Ariel walked in and sat down, uneasily, on the navy carpet. Flame's mobile phone beeped. She ignored it, but it beeped again; then Marina's phone beeped too. Ariel groaned.

Ash looked cross. 'Can you please turn off your phones for a mo,' she said. Flame and Marina turned off their phones again and put them down.

For what felt like a long time they were silent, then Flame said, 'I'm not sure what we should do.' Ash and Ariel gave each other a quick smile: their eldest sister hated not knowing what to do. Marina frowned: she knew Flame's admission meant that she was worried.

Ariel looked at Flame. 'Is that why you're in a such a bad mood?' she said.

Flame shot her little sister such a withering look that it seemed an argument would start, but Ash said quickly, 'We need to find out what these yellow-eyed things are and what they want.'

They settled back and nodded in agreement. Marina looked round at Ariel. 'What does Sidney say about them?'

Ariel blinked with surprise. 'I'd completely forgotten to ask him.'

Flame made a face as if to say, 'Well you should have done!'

'Could you go down now?' said Marina.

'I s'pose so,' said Ariel.

'Don't let Mum or Dad see you,' said Flame. 'We don't want them to start getting suspicious.'

'That was awkward with Dad about the scorch mark,' said Marina.

As Ariel got off the bed, Ash said, 'I'll come with you.'

With their left hands sliding along the banister rail, the two sisters ran down the wide mahogany staircase. The banister ended with a huge acorn-shaped newel post, which they liked to swing round. In the spacious hallway, at the bottom of the staircase, hung the portrait of Sidney Sprite and beside him the portrait of Mim, his wife. Both portraits were large with ornate gilt frames and were painted in 1910, the year that Sidney built Sprite Towers. Mim looked to be a pretty woman with lively eyes and dark hair piled up on her head. Sidney had reddish hair and a jolly, whiskery face. He looked the sort of man who would enjoy eating toffees and telling stories.

Ash slung her arm around the newel post and tilted her head towards the kitchen door, ready to alert Ariel. Ariel stood close to Sidney's portrait and started whispering. To Ash, Sidney's portrait appeared silent and immobile, but Ariel could hear her great-great-grandfather's voice and see his face changing as he spoke to her.

At first Ariel looked curious as she listened. Then, as she asked more questions and heard Sidney's replies, she gulped and began to look frightened. Finally, she whispered, 'Thank you, Sidney', to the portrait and turned to Ash with a face white as a sheet.

'What is it?' whispered Ash. Ariel stood speechless.

Chapter Ten
SCREEGLINGS

Ash looked round quickly at the kitchen door – all was quiet – then grabbed Ariel's arm and led her upstairs to Flame's bedroom. As they entered, the older girls saw Ariel's white face and were alarmed. Ash sat her little sister on the bed beside Marina, then climbed on too. The four sisters leaned back against the wall, shivering, until Flame said, 'Let's get under the duvet.' They clambered off, pulled back the red duvet, sat back down in a line against the wall and pulled the duvet over them. Warmer, but with a sense of growing unease, they waited. Between Ash and Marina, Ariel sat silently, staring ahead.

Then Marina said to her gently, 'What did Sidney say?'

'Screeglings,' whispered Ariel.

'Screeglings?'

'Screeglings?'

'Screeglings?'

'Yes, screeglings.'

Flame, Marina and Ash looked round from one to the other, their faces tense.

'What are they, Ariel?' said Ash, gently.

'They're evil.'

For a few seconds they were silent. The word 'evil' seemed to the sisters to echo around the room. They pulled up the duvet around them.

'And?' said Ash, gently.

'They're sort of half-insect and half-goblin.'

Marina shuddered. 'Yerrk.' Flame gulped. Ash whispered, 'They sound horrible.'

Still staring ahead, her eyes wide, Ariel whispered, 'Sidney said they creep around in the dark, then bury themselves in the ground in the day.'

'That's why you and Ash couldn't see them in the wood,' said Flame.

'The clicking sound must be their legs,' said Ash.

Marina groaned, 'That's minging.'

'How does Sidney know this?' asked Flame.

Ariel shook her head. 'Sidney knows everything that happens here.'

'But why have these things appeared now? Has he seen them before?'

'I didn't ask him if he'd seen them before. But he said we girls were not awake – that we had forgotten about our magic and Sprite Towers was no longer protected as it used to be.'

A cool draft blew through the open window.

The sisters shivered. For some time they were silent, absorbed in their thoughts. What Sidney had said was true: they had forgotten about their magic, especially since Mrs Duggery died. Grandma never spoke about it any more, as Ottalie had asked her to promise that she would not keep secrets.

Eventually, Flame said, 'So where do the screeglings come from?'

Ariel gave a big sigh. 'Sidney says that screeglings live deep in the earth, but they sometimes climb to the surface when they find an opening.'

'So, why have they come out now?' asked Flame.

'And where's this opening?' said Ash.

Ariel gulped and a tear rolled down her face. 'When… when I was flying …'

Flame's eyes narrowed. 'I knew it!'

'It's not my fault!' cried Ariel, with a sob.

'Sssh, Flame – stop it,' said Marina, putting out her hand. 'Let Ariel tell us what happened.' Flame blew out hard and leaned back against the wall.

'Ariel, don't forget to tell them about the person standing in the Wild Wood,' said Ash.

Flame and Marina looked hard at Ariel.

The youngest Sprite Sister took a deep breath. 'I told you – you know I told you! I saw someone standing on the track on Saturday night. Well, on

Monday night they were in the wood.'

'That's really creepy,' said Marina.

Flame groaned. 'Great. So we've got screeglings on the lawn and someone wandering around in the grounds.'

Ariel nodded. Ash murmured, 'Yes.' Marina buried her face in the duvet.

Flame rubbed her forehead. 'Start from the beginning, can you.'

Ariel drew another deep breath. With a sense of resolve, she wiped away her tears and said, 'The first night I flew, I came down too quickly and landed in the undergrowth, the other side of the wall.'

'Outside Sprite Towers?' said Marina. Ariel nodded.

'And?

'And I hit this big stone with my foot and hurt my ankle.'

'That's why you were limping the other day,' said Marina.

'Yes.'

'What's that got to do with the screeglings?' asked Flame.

'Sidney thinks that when I knocked the stone, it opened a hole in the ground.'

Flame frowned, then looked at Ariel. She sat back, thought for a few seconds, her face getting red, then she turned to Ariel and looked as if she was about to explode.

'You and your practising your magic – I knew it!'

'Hang on, Flame,' whispered Ash, fiercely, putting both hands out. 'Be fair – we're always knocking over stones and we haven't released a screegling up till now.'

'I can't see how I moved the stone much – it was huge,' said Ariel.

Flame breathed out loudly.

Ariel took a deep breath. 'This person I saw on the track, then in the Wild Wood – Sidney says he called up the screeglings.'

'Sidney says *he* called up the screeglings?' echoed Marina.

'Yes,' replied Ariel.

'Who is *he*?' asked Flame, catching her sister's eye.

Ariel was silent.

Marina leaned forward, 'Did Sidney tell you who *he* was?'

'No,' said Ariel, looking down, then glancing round at Ash.

'Why didn't Sidney tell you?' asked Marina.

'He didn't know,' said Ariel, crossing her fingers under the duvet, as she knew she was telling a fib. Sidney had told her, but Ariel knew instinctively that this was not the right time to tell Flame and Marina. She had whispered the name to Ash as they walked up the stairs. With a look of alarm, Ash had held up her finger to her mouth and whispered, 'Ssh,' and Ariel had nodded in agreement.

But the younger sisters had forgotten Flame's ability to see the truth in a situation, which came with her power of Fire. Now, she leaned forward and looked Ariel in the eye. Ariel blinked, had a sudden instinct of the question she knew would follow. In a soft voice, Flame said, 'Ariel, I know when you are lying. Please tell me who Sidney Sprite thought the figure was.'

Ariel looked at Ash. Ash looked at Ariel. They both looked at Flame, then at Marina. A tear rolled down Ariel's left cheek. They waited, then Flame said again, 'Ariel, who is he?'

'Sidney says ...'

'Yes?'

'Sidney says to beware of the boy with hawk-like eyes.'

For a moment, there was absolute silence. Nobody moved.

Marina looked round at Flame and Ash. 'The boy with hawk-like eyes?'

Still nobody said anything. Then, in a small voice, Ariel said, 'I think Sidney means Zak.'

Marina drew in a sharp breath. '*Zak?*' she said, pushing herself forward and away from her sisters. 'But, but – he's a *friend!*'

114

Ariel nodded and drew the duvet up as far as she could. She felt tired now.

'I don't understand,' said Marina.

'Nor do I,' said Ariel.

Flame's face was thoughtful. 'Whatever has Zak got to do with this? How is he connected?'

Ariel looked round at eldest sister with a weary, teary face. 'I don't know – but what I'm trying to say is that the screeglings are not just my fault. I might have knocked against the stone, but there's someone else involved.'

For a second, the youngest and the eldest Sprite Sisters held each other's gaze. Then Flame nodded and sat back against the wall. Marina leaned back. Ariel clasped the duvet tight. Ash, cross-legged, leant her chin on her hands.

Flame broke the silence. 'So, is Zak somehow controlling the screeglings?'

'I don't know – that's all Sidney said about him,' replied Ariel. 'I was a bit upset by then.'

Flame's expression softened and they were silent again. After a while, Flame said, 'So, just going back a bit, did Sidney tell you what he thought the screeglings would do?'

Ariel drew a large breath and her face tensed. They waited – then she whispered, 'This is the worst bit.'

Marina groaned. 'What, there's more? I don't believe it!'

Flame bit her lip, her eyes worried. Ash shivered.

'What does he say?' said Flame.

Ariel took a big breath and blurted, 'Sidney thinks the screeglings may try to invade the house.'

'No!' cried Marina, sitting bolt upright. 'Not insects crawling through the house – I can't bear it!'

'Sssh, Marina! Calm down!' said Flame, but their hearts were beating fast now and their faces tense as they looked from one to the other.

'Apparently the screeglings get in through the nooks and crannies,' said Ariel.

Marina looked as if she was going to be sick. She clambered off the bed, walked across the room, her body rigid with tension. 'I really hate things that crawl about,' she whimpered. 'It's disgusting.'

'Screeglings in the *house*?' said Ash, with a shudder. 'That's *horrible* …'

They were silent. The only noise came from the faint ticking of Flame's bedside clock. A chilly draft blew around the bedroom. The sisters shivered.

Flame looked across at Ariel and said, 'Is there anything else you can think of that Sidney told you?'

Ariel thought for a moment, then she whispered, 'Yes.'

'And?'

'He said – he said that screeglings poison the air.'

Flame gasped. The thought of the screeglings crawling through the house had made her feel icy cold, but now she thought her heart might come through her chest. *'Poison the air?'* she said, in a voice that sounded half-strangled.

Ariel and Flame held each other's gaze, their eyes wide with fear and their hearts pounding. White-faced, Marina felt herself reeling and reached for the wall. Ash began to shiver hard, feeling a chill right through her body. No one spoke or moved. In the sky, dark clouds began to gather and the wind blew around Sprite Towers.

In a small voice, Ariel said, 'I told you it was evil magic.'

The silence that fell now felt so heavy the sisters felt as if they might never move. Eventually Marina said, 'Our magic power had no effect on the screeglings last night. Are we going to be able to stop them getting into the house?'

Her three sisters looked as confused as if someone had clonked them over the head.

'We don't know, do we?' said Marina, her voice rising.

Flame shook her head. 'It's too much to take in.'

'But we can't just hang about up here,' said Marina.

117

'The screeglings might be really close to the house by now.'

Ariel pushed off the duvet and climbed off the bed. 'We need to practise and strengthen our magic powers,' she said. 'That's what we ought to do first.'

Flame and Ash got off the bed. For a few seconds the Sprite Sisters stood, shaky and nervous, trying to get their balance.

Ariel moved to the door and pulled it open. 'Come on,' she said. 'Come on.'

Chapter Eleven
INVASION

The Sprite Sisters ran down the stairs and through the hallway to the kitchen. At the door Ariel turned, her face white. 'Can you smell it?'

'Please don't let the screeglings already be here,' cried Marina, putting her hand over her mouth.

'Too late,' said Flame, as Ariel opened the door. Behind her, Marina gave a little cry.

The smell hit them like a smack in the face. It was a terrible smell – the smell of putrefying flesh. They walked into the kitchen holding their noses and covering their mouths. The windows and the door were wide open. By the table, Ottalie stood, frazzled and pale. 'Ah, there you all are. I wondered where you'd all got to.'

'We've been in Flame's room,' said Ash. Ottalie blinked with surprise.

'Are you alright, Mum?' asked Flame, alarmed by her mother's appearance.

'It's this smell,' said Ottalie, holding her forehead. 'It's making me feel ill. We've been trying to work out where it's coming from.'

'Phyerrgh – it stinks,' said Ariel.

In the far corner Colin was crouched down on the floor, peering behind the dishwasher. Archie paced up and down, sniffing and growling.

The Sprite Sisters looked from one to another with horrified faces.

Colin pulled himself up. 'I've checked behind all the cupboards and there are no dead mice. It must be coming from the drains – a blockage, perhaps.' As he spoke, his eyes were on Archie. 'What's up with him? There's something he doesn't like.'

Marina stood behind her sisters, looking around the floor, her face white. Every few seconds, she made a little squeak of panic. Ash moved beside her and whispered, 'Sssh.'

'Well, we'd better get someone to look at it,' said Ottalie. 'I need some fresh air.'

'Me too – my head is pounding,' said Colin. They all walked to the open back door and filed out.

The Sprite Sisters stared at their parents, as they leaned against the brick wall.

'Ah, fresh air,' gasped Ottalie. Beside her, Colin coughed and spluttered.

'We'll take Archie down to the camp,' said Flame. 'Come on, boy.'

Their parents watched as their daughters ran over the lawn together.

'How long is it since we've seen them do that?' said Ottalie, with a pang of sadness. Colin put his arm around her shoulders and kissed her on the side of the face. 'A long time,' he said, softly.

'It seems like only yesterday that they were little,' said Ottalie.

'And we were young,' said Colin, with a smile. The next moment, he clasped his forehead. 'I don't feel very well.'

'Funny you should say that,' said Ottalie. 'I feel queasy, too.'

'Must be that blasted stench,' said Colin. 'It's poisoned us.'

Holding her head, Ottalie said, 'I think I might go and lie down.'

'I'll come with you,' said Colin, his face turning a pale green.

At the camp, Ariel and Ash flopped down on chairs by the campfire while Flame and Marina stood, looking around.

Ash looked up at the sky and said, 'The clouds are getting dark – looks like we could be in for a storm.'

Ariel nodded.

'I haven't been down here all summer,' said Flame, looking at the old white caravan.

'Nor me,' said Marina.

'Come on, you two, time is pressing,' called Ash. Flame and Marina pulled up chairs and sat down with their sisters. All four girls had tense, worried faces.

'Mum looked terrible,' said Flame.

'So did Dad,' said Ash.

'They've been poisoned,' said Ariel.

'But the smell was only in the kitchen, wasn't it?' said Flame. 'We didn't smell it anywhere else.'

'Maybe we've got time to stop the screeglings getting any further through the house,' said Ash.

'I can't go in with those screegle things there,' moaned Marina. 'I can't bear it to think of them creeping about. I shall be sick – and then I'd be no help. I'll go and stay with Janey or Su-Ling.'

'You can't do that,' said Flame, in her bossy voice. 'We need you to help us get rid of the screeglings.'

'Well, I can't help!' cried Marina. 'I'm sure they're crawling down my back – I can feel them.'

'You've got to help – we don't have any choice in this.'

'Surely they're not small enough to crawl down our backs,' said Ash, almost to herself.

Flame leaned forward. 'What size are they, do you think?'

Ash sat up in her chair. 'Their eyes are big enough

122

to be seen across the lawn – so they must be quite big. On the other hand, they're small enough to crawl through cracks and crannies, which would mean they were tiny. So … I don't know …'

Flame stared ahead. 'It's bizarre,' she murmured.

'Basically, we haven't got a clue,' said Marina.

They were silent for a while, deliberating on this conundrum.

Ariel gazed straight ahead, her face thoughtful. Suddenly she said, 'Perhaps the screeglings' magic allows them to change size and grow bigger or smaller.'

'Errgh,' groaned Marina. 'I can't bear it another minute.'

'Shut up, Marina,' snapped Flame, but she looked at Ariel with admiration. It was not the first time that her little sister had clarified a situation with one of her insights.

'So, we're possibly dealing with things that can change shape,' said Ash.

Ariel's eyes opened wide. 'They might grow huge!'

Marina groaned again and pulled her mobile phone out of her pocket. 'I've had 21 texts since we started talking this morning,' she said, looking at the screen.

'Any from Zak?' asked Ariel.

'Yeah – three,' replied Marina.

'Don't reply to him, Marina!' said Ariel.

'Let them all wait, please,' said Ash.

Marina put her mobile back in her pocket. Her face tensed as she said, 'I don't want to think about screeglings.'

'Well, you've got to,' said Flame. 'We've all got to.'

'We need you,' said Ariel.

'I don't understand why you're blaming Zak,' said Marina.

Flame began to look cross. 'We don't know if Zak is connected and, if he is, how he is. We can sort that out later. The first thing we've got to do is get these horrible things out of our house.'

Ariel looked thoughtful. 'Except, we don't know if Zak could call them out.'

Flame looked flustered. 'Yeah, that's true. Oh dear, where do we start …'

'We always start with the Circle of Power,' said Ash.

Marina bit her lip. 'We know our magic is wonky because we couldn't make the Circle of Power last night. Perhaps we should start by trying to fix that.'

'That's it,' said Ash, getting up. 'Come on – we can't do anything till we know we can use our powers together.'

'I just hope Mum and Dad don't come barging in,' said Flame.

'I doubt it, looking at the colour of Dad's face,' said Ash.

In the middle of the camp, they stood in a circle. With their distinct colourings the four sisters had always looked different from each other, but when they were younger this was less marked. Now they looked a completely disparate group. Flame towered over them, with the athletic body and long legs she'd inherited from her grandmother, Marilyn, along with her green eyes and copper hair. Opposite her, at the west of the circle, stood Ash. She had her father's chestnut hair and brown eyes and would grow to be tall; she was gaining height now she was nearly 13, but had a long way to go to catch up with Flame. At the south of the circle stood Marina. Tall and strong, she was athletic but had broader shoulders. Marina had inherited her grandfather Sheldon Sprite's blue eyes and dark, curly hair.

Standing at the north, Ariel had her mother's petite figure, wavy blonde hair and big grey eyes. She looked tiny beside her older sisters – like a little angel beside three giants. Her sisters knew otherwise. Of them all, it was Ariel and her curiosity that had the potential to get them into trouble.

What happened next surprised them all.

There was something – perhaps habit or familiarity – in the back of their minds that made them feel that, when they really focused, their magic powers would be equal and balanced as they had always been. As they took each other's hands and closed their eyes, they expected to feel the circle of blue light around them.

What actually happened was that Ariel's power was so much stronger than the rest of them, she almost knocked her sisters over. Instead of creating a ring of blue light around them, Ariel generated a huge ball of light that fizzed through their fingers and whooshed around them. They opened their eyes, dropped their hands and stared at each other in astonishment.

'Ow!' cried Ash and Marina.

'Flipping heck, Ariel!' said Flame, shaking her hands and stepping back.

Ariel looked sheepish. 'I'm sorry – I didn't mean to hurt you. I think my power has got a lot stronger.'

'Telling me,' muttered Flame.

Ash said, 'You don't need to feel sorry.'

Marina looked across at Ariel and said, 'Did you really fly over Sprite Towers?'

Ariel smiled. 'Yes.'

'What did it feel like?'

'It was absolutely amazing.'

Marina had a dreamy look on her face. 'I'll bet.'

Flame stepped forward again. 'Ariel, how did you do it? I mean, how did you make *yourself* lift? It must have been different from pointing your finger at an object and making that rise up.'

'It was difficult at first,' said Ariel. 'I couldn't see how to do it. Then I realised I had to imagine it and feel it.'

'And it worked?' said Flame.

Ariel giggled. 'I practised in the tower before I went outside. Mum came in, looking for me, and I was hovering up near the ceiling. I was praying she wouldn't look up. I knew if I lost my concentration, I'd crash to the floor. Thankfully, she didn't see me.'

The older girls smiled at this and for a second, they were silent. Then Ariel continued, 'I could feel my magic had got a lot stronger.' She looked round at each of her sisters. 'I wanted to use it: I felt I *had* to, that it was part of me and I didn't want to let it go.'

'Use it or lose it, they say,' said Flame.

'But now we can't make the Circle of Power,' said Marina.

Ariel shrugged. 'I can try to pull back my power, but really you should all practise to strengthen your powers. That way our power would be balanced again, as well as stronger.'

'I have been practising a little,' said Ash.

Flame looked across at her. 'You too! Anything else we ought to know?'

Ariel and Ash looked at one another, then at Flame. 'No,' they both said.

'It's not our fault you don't want to use your magic any more,' said Ariel.

'Who said I didn't?'

Ash shrugged. 'C'mon, be fair, Flame – you've had other things on your mind.'

Flame snorted. 'Well, I don't have a lot of choice now, with the house full of screeglings.'

'Then practise your power,' said Ariel. 'Do what I did – then maybe we can make the Circle of Power and get started.'

Marina pulled her mobile phone out of her pocket and stared at the screen. 'I haven't answered my mobile all morning. People will begin to wonder if I'm all right.'

'Marina, wise up!' said Ash, infuriated. 'The house is full of screeglings. The air is being poisoned as we stand here. Stop wasting time worrying about your blasted texts!'

Marina frowned and shoved the mobile back in her pocket. 'Sorry,' she mumbled.

Ariel stood with her hands on her hips and said, 'Find somewhere where you'll be out of sight and get practising. Go on!'

'What are you going to do?' asked Flame.

'I'm going up to the house, to see what's

happening,' said Ariel. 'I'll take Archie, so you'll have some peace.'

For the next hour, Flame, Marina and Ash practised their magic powers. Flame stood in the stable yard and was hidden from view by the big wall that surrounded it. Ash went into the vegetable garden and was hidden by the high beech hedge. Marina walked to the Secret Garden at the end of the tennis court. Having done a little practice already, Ash felt familiar with the feeling of power surging through her fingers. For Flame and Marina, it came as a shock. Both were surprised by the strength of their power – even more so than they had been the night before – and both had to practise hard to control it. This new power had a sprawling, wayward quality and both sisters recognised that for it to be of any use, it would need to be controlled.

Flame worked on focusing her power of Fire to be as precise and fine as a laser beam. She also thought about fire as having the power to consume and renew. If the screeglings came from deep within the earth, they would be inured to heat at a tremendous temperature, she reasoned. Could she transform them through her power of Fire? For the moment, she did not know, but she carried on practising.

In the Secret Garden, Marina practised her power of Water and learned a way to send a needle of ice so cold and so sharp that it would burn a hole through anything it touched. If the screeglings grew bigger she would freeze them in their tracks, she decided.

In the vegetable garden, Ash practised her power of Earth. The more she practised, the more refined her power became and she found she was able to bind something as small as one blade of grass to another, with absolute precision. If she used her power on a screegling now, even if it changed its shape, she felt it would never be able to completely escape: some part of it would be fixed and immobile. Next, she wondered about shrinking things and began to practise that.

Meanwhile, in the house, Ariel shut Archie in the utility room (having opened the window), then ran from room to room, up and down, opening windows. Some of the big sash windows on the ground floor would not budge and she was not tall enough to lift them. She would leave those for Flame and Marina to tackle, but soon fresh air blew through the house. Where are Mum and Dad, wondered Ariel. She ran up to their bedroom and knocked on the door. 'Come in,' called her mother and she entered to find her parents lying on their bed with pale faces.

'We're not feeling very well, love,' said Ottalie.

'But you're never ill,' said Ariel. She sat down on the side of the bed and took her mother's hand. 'Can

I get you anything?'

'Just some water, please,' said her mother. Beside her, Colin groaned. He pulled himself up and staggered to the bathroom at the side of the room.

'We're both feeling a bit sick,' said Ottalie.

'I'll be back in a minute,' said Ariel and hurried out of the room. As quickly as she could, she got two glasses of water from the kitchen and carried them up to the bedroom. 'Is there anything else you need?'

Ottalie shook her head. Colin was still in the bathroom.

'I'll be back soon,' said Ariel, shutting the door. Then she ran from room to room, looking for yellow eyes and signs of movement – anything that might show her where the screeglings were hidden – but she could see nothing. The only sign was the terrible putrid smell wafting through the house – which was now being carried by the air blowing through.

A minute later, Ariel ran to find her sisters. To each one, she panted breathlessly, 'We must hurry – Mum and Dad are in bed and feeling really ill. The screeglings are poisoning the air!'

Chapter Twelve
TENSION

The Sprite Sisters charged up to the house and burst in through the back door. The smell hit them, even though the windows were wide open. Screwing up their faces, they looked round the kitchen with a sense of disgust. Marina reached out to steady herself on the table.

Flame started to open cupboards and peer inside. 'I loathe the idea of the screeglings in our house, but I wish I could see one. Where are they?'

'They're here somewhere,' said Ash, peering into the bread bin.

'Ergh, not in our food,' moaned Marina.

From the pantry Ariel called out, 'Do you think screeglings like any particular food?'

'We could put out some bait,' said Ash, walking in behind her.

While the younger sisters debated what screeglings might eat, Marina clung miserably to the kitchen table.

Flame walked to the door. 'I'm going to see if Mum and Dad are okay.' She returned a few minutes later, filled the kettle and set it on the Aga to boil. 'They're no better. I'm going to make them hot water bottles as they're feeling cold and shivery.'

'Oh dear,' said Ash.

'If we don't hurry up and get rid of the screeglings, we'll be ill too,' muttered Flame, pulling out a water jug from a cupboard.

'We're all going to die of poisoning,' said Marina.

'For heaven's sakes, Marina, pull yourself together and do something useful,' snapped Flame.

'I don't want to look for screeglings.'

'Then open some of the big windows. Ash, help her – and Ariel, get out the hotties from the cupboard.'

As she waited for the kettle to boil, Flame filled a water jug. As soon as the hot water bottles were ready, she and Ariel carried everything up the stairs.

'Do you think our magic powers will protect us against being poisoned?' asked Ariel, holding the hotties against her chest.

'I hope so,' said Flame, holding the water jug. As she listened to Ariel, she wondered if should phone Quinn: she hadn't talked to him yet. Behind her, Ariel asked, 'How many screeglings do you think there are?'

'I don't know,' replied Flame, trying to focus her mind. 'Could be hundreds, I suppose.'

'Maybe thousands …' Ariel shivered at the thought of this.

As they entered their parents' bedroom, Flame put down the jug and went to open the window. 'Don't open that – I'm freezing,' said Ottalie, white-faced and shivering. Flame hesitated. 'Just a little bit, Mum,' she said. 'It's stuffy in here. The hot water bottles will help you and Dad warm up a bit.'

Ottalie Sprite smiled weakly at her daughters. 'Thank you, girls,' she said, taking a hot water bottle and holding it against her. 'I don't know what's got into us.' Beside her on the bed, Colin Sprite groaned.

'You must stay up here and keep warm,' said Flame.

'You must stay in bed,' echoed Ariel.

As soon as they managed to reassure their mother that they would all be fine, they left the room and joined their sisters in the drawing room.

'We've opened the dining room windows,' said Marina.

'The wind's getting up,' said Ash, watching dark clouds scud across the sky.

'Looks like we'll have a storm soon,' said Flame. 'We'll need to get the windows shut quickly when it comes.' She walked to the side of the room by the fireplace, then bent down. Here, the polished oak floorboards were widely spaced. 'The screeglings could be coming in through the cracks,' she said, and peered down into one.

'They could be right through the house by now,' said Marina.

'Can you smell anything in here?' asked Ariel, peering under the sofa.

'Not so much now with the windows open,' said Ash.

'I know the wind's rising, but we'd better open some windows upstairs,' said Flame.

For the next ten minutes the four sisters opened as many windows as would budge. As the sky darkened, cool air swirled around Sprite Towers.

'Mum and Dad will have a fit if they come out and see all these windows open,' said Ariel, as they opened the last window in the attic. 'What will we say?'

'I don't know,' replied Flame. 'We must make sure they stay in their room.'

'Dad didn't look as if he was going anywhere except the bathroom in a hurry,' said Ariel.

'Okay, so the windows are open and the house is freezing – now what do we do?' said Marina.

'Circle of Power,' said Ash.

'Whereabouts?' said Ariel.

'We need to keep the magic in the house,' said Marina.

'Drawing room,' suggested Flame.

Stopping to check their parents were still in bed and had everything they needed, the sisters made their way downstairs. In the drawing room, they pushed back the two cream sofas and stood on the rug in the middle of the room. Confident they would quickly create the Circle of Power after that day's practice, they took hold of each other's hands and shut their eyes. As they called in their magic power, a line of blue light circled round them – wavered, wobbled and petered out.

'What's wrong?' they chorused.

'We've always been able to make the Circle of Power!' said Marina.

Ash frowned. 'I think we're pushing against one another.'

They tried again, this time restraining their power. Again, the Circle of Power appeared, but again it sputtered out.

'I can't feel it,' said Ariel.

'What's wrong?' asked Ash, bewildered.

They all looked at one another, with the same thought. 'Perhaps the screeglings are affecting our powers,' said Flame. Her face looked worried and drawn.

'That's true – they could be,' said Ash.

For a moment they were silent, listening for the sound of scuttling insects.

Marina shivered.

'Let's try again,' said Flame.

For the third time, the Sprite Sisters took each other's hands and tried to create the Circle of Power. This time a much stronger circle of blue light appeared around them. For a few seconds, their faces relaxed with relief, then tightened as the light began to change shape. Instead of a smooth blue light, the circle became bulbous at one side and thin at the other.

The sisters dropped their hands in despair.

'I don't understand – my power of Fire was strong when I practised earlier,' said Flame.

'So was my power of Water,' said Marina.

Ash stared at her hands. 'We're all right individually.'

'It's the collective we can't manage,' said Flame.

'So it's something about us working together,' said Marina.

'We're not connected like we used to be,' said Ariel.

The four of them slumped, their faces tense with worry. 'While we dither about, the screeglings are crawling further into our house,' said Flame.

'And Mum and Dad are sick,' said Ariel.

They were silent. Marina shivered, crossed her arms and rubbed her hands up and down.

'There's something we used to do, that we're not doing now,' said Flame.

'It's something we didn't think about or we'd know what it was,' said Ash.

Ariel frowned and looked hard at Flame. 'I think

the problem is you and Marina.'

'Oh, don't be so daft, Ariel,' replied Flame.

'Ash and I haven't changed,' said Ariel. 'It's you who've changed.'

'We've *all* changed,' said Marina.

'Well, you've changed more than we have,' said Ariel. 'Neither you nor Flame cared about your magic until the screeglings came.'

'That's a stupid thing to say!' said Flame, her colour rising.

'It's true! You haven't talked about our magic power for *ages*,' said Ariel.

Flame bit her lip, knew this to be true.

Marina turned away, angrily, and for a few seconds it seemed as if one of them would storm out.

Ash said, 'It's not a competition! The house is full of disgusting insects that are polluting the air and making Mum and Dad ill. This is no time to argue.'

'But our magic isn't going to work till we've sorted this out,' said Ariel.

They were silent again. Flame turned and walked to one of the sofas and sank down onto it. The others followed. They all stared moodily at the floor.

'It feels like we keep having the same discussion,' said Marina.

Ariel spat out, 'I don't know why you and Flame

can't admit that you don't want to be a part of us, the Sprite Sisters, any longer.'

Flame shot Ariel a withering look and flicked back her long copper hair, 'How ridiculous,' she said. 'I don't know why you don't admit that you were out of line in going off and learning to fly.'

'That's got nothing to do with it!' shouted Ariel.

Flame scoffed. 'No? Well what about letting out the screeglings then? We might not be in this horrible dilemma if you hadn't gone flapping about all over Sprite Towers and knocking over stones!'

'Zak let the screeglings out, not me!'

Marina turned and looked as if she was about to wade into the argument, and Flame was drawing breath, as Ash put out her hands, palms down, and said, 'Hey, hey – *please*. Let's just calm down. We don't know how the screeglings got here or why they're here.' She waited until her sisters had sat back, then she said, 'Let's focus on making the Circle of Power.'

Another silence followed.

'It feels like a chasm,' said Ariel, in a small voice.

'What?' asked Ash.

'The space between us,' said Ariel. 'I can feel it getting wider as we sit here.' She turned to look at Flame. 'I never know where I am with you these days. One minute you're okay, but the next you're biting my head off – and when you're like that you're *horrible*. And now, while we're sitting here with this thing we've got to sort out, it still feels like you're here in body but you're not really *present*. It's as if a part of your mind is still thinking about Quinn and all that stuff.'

'That's what happens when you grow up,' retorted Flame.

Ariel looked at Marina, who was staring at the carpet. 'Marina is miles away,' she said.

'I'm listening, but I feel really uncomfortable with these things crawling round our house,' said Marina. 'To tell the truth, I *would* rather be talking to my friends right now.'

Ariel looked at Flame and Marina. 'Do you think you two could just be one of *us*, the Sprite Sisters, for a little while? Then you can go back to being Quinn's girlfriend and Miss Ever-So-Popular.'

Flame gave an exasperated look upwards. Marina made a scornful expression. As the tension rose again, Ash said quickly, 'I think Ariel is right. It's about being present with our hearts as well as our minds.'

Flame blew out hard. 'I thought we were.'

Ash smiled. 'Not enough to make the Circle of Power, it seems.' Flame gave her a small smile.

Marina turned towards them. 'All right then,' she said, but instead of leaping up and into action, the four

140

sisters sat silent.

Have we changed that much, each of them wondered. How is it that the times we played together and used our magic power feel so far away? All those amazing adventures we had fighting Glenda Glass … we were so close then …

Ariel finally broke the silence. With a sad look in her eyes, she said, 'We still care about one another – don't we? We might not like each other much at the moment, but we must still *care*. Surely.' A tear trickled down her cheek.

Flame and Marina swallowed hard. 'Yes, of course we care, you numpty,' they said to Ariel and they moved together on the sofa so that they sat in a big sisterly hug.

'I'm sorry,' said Flame. 'I'll try to be nicer to you.'

'Me too,' said Marina, wiping away a tear.

'And I'm sorry if my experiment with flying has made the screeglings come out,' said Ariel, with a loud sniff.

Ash, calm and steady, brushed away a tear and held her sisters tight; but they were not to sit there long. The moment was broken by a heavy rumble of thunder, followed by a crack of lightning.

They moved apart and rubbed their faces, then laughed. 'To work,' said Flame.

'To work,' echoed her sisters.

Chapter Thirteen
ENCOUNTER

The first sight they had of a screegling was a pair of legs disappearing between a crack in the drawing room floorboards. The legs were visible for only a split second, but Ariel was quick and her eyesight pin sharp in the darkened room. As thunder rumbled over the old house, the sisters were about to try to make the Circle of Power for the fourth time that day, but the faint sound of clicking alerted the youngest Sprite. Ariel had inherited her mother's exceptional hearing and in the nick of time she turned to see the screegling. 'There's one! I saw it!' she cried out and they rushed to look.

'What did you see? What did it look like? How big was it?'

'Black, er – sort of jointed.'

'Big?'

'Yes, I think so.'

'Like a locust?'

'Or a cockroach?'

'I dunno. Why?'

'Cockroaches really suck.'

'How big were the legs?'

Ariel frowned. She put out her hands and moved

them apart, then together. 'About this big,' she said, indicating something the size of tube of toothpaste.

Marina winced. 'Ergh, that's huge.'

'Well, it's gone now,' said Ash. She turned and looked down at the floor, then peered more closely. 'Hang on – there's some kind of slime down here.'

'Yuk, it smells,' said Ariel.

'It's a slime trail,' said Ash.

'Don't touch it,' said Flame. 'It may be poisonous.'

Ariel jumped back. 'That's gross.'

Marina shuddered. 'I can't bear the idea that the house is crawling with these horrible things.'

'Swarming through every bit of the house,' said Ariel.

'The thought that these things are watching us freaks me out,' said Ash. She pulled her magic stone out of her pocket and held it in her open palm. The stone glowed a sickly yellow. 'We can use this to guide us. It may save some time.'

'We need a plan,' said Flame.

'You and your plans,' said Ariel.

'I thought the plan was to start with the Circle of Power,' said Marina.

'It is.'

'So, come on then.'

They moved, once again, to form their circle on the

carpet: Flame at the east, Marina at the south, Ash at the west and Ariel at the north. As they took hold of each other's hands and closed their eyes, Flame murmured, 'Fire, Water, Earth and Air. We come together: four sisters, four elements, one power.'

The Sprite Sisters breathed into their magic. Within a few seconds a circle of blue light whooshed around them. This time the light was bright and strong and rose quickly around and below them until it formed a sphere. The Sprite Sisters were enclosed in a ball of dazzling blue light that became a white light – then a red light, then orange, yellow, green and once more into blue, until it melded into a rainbow of colours. As if of one mind, they opened their eyes and marvelled at the sphere of rainbow light around them.

'Now we're connected,' said Ariel, with a smile.

'Let's send the light through the house,' said Marina.

They shut their eyes again and imagined the ball of rainbow light growing bigger and bigger. They saw it pass through the old timbers and the plaster, through the furniture, the floorboards and carpets, through each of the rooms right up to the attics and down to the cellars. They imagined the light expanding still further until it covered the whole of Sprite Towers.

The light sustained for a short time only. As it began

to diminish, the four sisters opened their eyes. They stood in the circle until the light had completely faded, then they let go of each other's hands and stepped back, smiling and slightly dazed.

'That was better,' said Ariel.

'Certainly an improvement on our previous efforts,' said Flame, her face troubled. 'But the light faded too quickly: we're still not at full strength with our power.'

They all made for one of the big cream sofas and flopped down on it, exhausted. For the next few minutes, they regained their focus on the objects around them.

'I keep hearing the phone ring,' said Ash, craning her ear. 'I hope Mum and Dad can't hear it. They'll wonder where we are.'

'Better go and see if there's anything they want,' said Marina, getting up.

'I'll come with you,' said Flame.

'Me too,' said Ash.

'Then we begin the hunt for the screeglings,' said Ariel, following.

'And this time, there is no escape,' added Ash.

The girls took the stairs two by two. Outside, the storm moved off, but cool air whistled up the big staircase from the open windows.

With her long legs, Flame arrived first at their parents' bedroom door. 'I still think we need a plan,' she whispered. 'I mean, what are we going to do with the screeglings?'

'Blast them to smithereens, of course,' whispered Ariel.

'We could collect them up and put them back in the hole,' said Ash.

Marina groaned. 'That's a terrible idea. We'd have to touch them. No way.'

'Sssh now,' whispered Flame, turning the handle and opening the door.

Ottalie and Colin Sprite's bedroom had a high ceiling, cream walls and curtains and a pale brown carpet. Today, there was a distinct chill. Ottalie and Colin lay asleep, huddled under the duvet. To their daughters, they suddenly looked vulnerable. Flame walked to the sash window and closed it. Crowding round the bed, the sisters said, softly, 'Mum? Dad?' Ottalie and Colin woke up, pale-faced and shivering. 'How are you feeling?' their daughters asked.

Ottalie gave them a wan smile. 'Bit better, thank you. Really ought to get up now.'

'No, no, you mustn't get up,' the girls echoed one another. 'Everything is fine, honestly.'

'Is there anything you need?' asked Flame.

Ottalie shook her head. 'I don't think so, thank you.'

Ash sat down on the bed beside her father. Colin

gave her a bleary smile. 'I can't remember the last time I was ill in bed – must be years ago. Ought to get up now.'

'No, Dad, you must stay here and keep warm,' said Flame in her bossy voice. 'You're not well enough to get up. We don't want your germs!'

'Flame's right,' said Ash, taking her father's hand in hers.

'Okay, love,' he said, wearily.

Sitting beside her mother, Ariel said, 'We've had a storm.'

'Yes, I heard the thunder,' said Ottalie.

'Have you closed the windows?' said Colin.

'Will do, Dad,' said Flame.

'Is that terrible smell still down there?'

'Yes, a bit – but not so much,' replied Flame. 'Don't worry. Just get better. We'll be back in a while.'

As the girls moved towards the door, Ottalie called, 'Don't forget to feed Archie and Pudding.'

'No, we won't Mum – just rest,' said Ariel, as she closed the door behind her. 'Wait,' she called to her sisters at the top of the staircase. They turned back and saw her anxious face. 'Do you think there any screeglings in Mum and Dad's room?'

They shivered at the thought of this.

'My stone didn't light up,' said Ash. 'I think their

room may be clear of screeglings for the moment.'

'Thank heavens for that,' said Flame. 'Come on, let's feed the animals and we can get going.'

As they ran down the wide mahogany staircase, Marina said, 'If the putrid smell has subsided, which it has for the moment, Mum and Dad might not be ill for much longer.'

'I was thinking that,' said Flame.

'But if we wait till dark, we might see the screeglings,' said Ash.

'They're all around us, watching us with their big yellow eyes, clicking their horrible legs,' said Ariel.

Marina shuddered again. 'Stop it, Ariel.' She walked towards the kitchen door and the others followed.

A few minutes later, Archie and Pudding were fed and the sisters sat at the table, drinking glasses of juice and eating slices of their mother's homemade fruitcake.

'That's better,' said Flame. 'I was so hungry.'

'Me too,' said Marina.

'Why do you think Mum and Dad were more affected by the smell than us?' asked Ash, through a mouthful of cake.

'Good question,' said Flame.

'They're never ill, but they're pole-axed,' said Ash.

'Perhaps our magic gives us some protection,' said Marina.

'Could be, or perhaps it was that they were trying to find the source of the smell and breathed in more of it than we have,' said Flame.

'Maybe grown-ups are more susceptible to the smell of screeglings,' said Ariel with a shrug.

'It doesn't smell in here now,' said Ash.

'That's because it's like a wind tunnel with the back door open,' said Flame.

'It might come back any minute,' said Ariel.

'Then try using your power of Air to clear it,' said Ash.

'Yep,' agreed Ariel.

As soon as they finished, the Sprite Sisters began the process of shutting windows through the rest of the house. The smell of the screeglings had subsided, but if their parents got up now there would be a lot of explaining to do. Working their way up the house, they finally arrived at the attics.

'Do you suppose that the screeglings' power will be diminished by us making that Circle of Power and sending the light through the house?' asked Ash, closing the metal handle on a rusty casement window.

'Yes, it must be – surely,' replied Flame.

'If they have evil magic, it might not touch them,' said Ash.

Flame looked thoughtful. 'Our magic was powerful,

so I'm sure it will have affected them.' But as she said this, a note of alarm rang in her mind. Sidney told Ariel the screeglings were half-goblin and half-insect. That's a pretty nasty combination, she thought to herself. For a second she was lost in the sense that they might already be out of their depth.

'I hope you're right,' Ash was saying, as Flame came to and focused her mind. 'Right, we're done, windows all shut. Let's get going.'

Ariel crouched down close to the floor, peering through a crack in the floorboards.

'Careful a screegling doesn't jump up and bite you,' said Marina.

Ariel jumped back. 'Ergh, don't say that!'

Marina grabbed an old broom that was lying on the floor and brushed away a big cobweb. 'Why don't we start up here and work downwards,' she said, peering into the corner.

'It's the right direction,' said Ash. 'If the screeglings live in the earth, they should be sent back to it.'

'I was thinking more of gravity,' said Marina. 'I could use my power to flush through the pipes. Wash the screeglings away.'

'Are they in the pipes?' asked Ariel, screwing up her nose.

'I don't know – they may be,' said Marina. 'They

could be everywhere. I think we could use our powers to push them down through the house. I can blast them with water, you with air. Ash can bind them down.'

'And bind the places where we've cleaned them out, so they don't come back,' added Ash.

Flame looked around, scratching her head. 'I'm not sure if things that live in the earth's crust will be affected by fire …'

'Use your power like a laser, remember?' said Ash. 'If you see a screegling send it a fine beam of your power.'

Flame nodded. 'I could try that.'

'You can't mess about with evil magic,' said Ariel. 'If we don't get rid of the screeglings, they may drive *us* out of the house.'

'Stop it, Ariel,' said Marina. 'It won't come to that.'

'But it could!' protested Ariel.

'I agree,' said Flame.

'Sidney told Ariel the screeglings were evil,' said Ash. 'My magic stone confirms it. I don't like killing things, but I don't see that we have a choice.'

Marina sighed. 'I shall be pleased when this is all over.'

'Sssh,' whispered Flame and pointed to the floor. They stood still and listened. The faint sound of clicking came from the gap in the floorboards that Ariel had been examining. Ash moved quietly towards it and crouched down. She held out her right hand, to use her power of Earth to sense if there was a screegling beneath the floorboards. Flame, Marina and Ariel waited, their hearts pumping fast.

'I wonder if I can get it out, so we can have a look at it,' said Ash.

'No, no, don't do that,' groaned Marina. 'I don't want to see it. Just deal with it there.'

Ariel's eyes grew wide. 'If the screeglings come out and grow huge, they could eat us alive.'

Flame and Marina threw up their hands. *'Ariel, shut up!'* said Marina.

'Huh,' said Ariel, putting her nose in the air.

Still crouched on the floor, Ash said in a thoughtful voice, 'If I bind it so it can never move and it dies up here, it will smell till it's rotted down.'

'Well, bind it so much that it won't smell!' said Marina.

'We don't know if dead screeglings do rot down,' said Flame. 'If they've got evil magic, they could transform themselves into something else.'

Ash lifted her right hand and pointed her finger. There was a flash of bright blue light, then another, as she sent her magic power of Earth to bind the screegling. Peering into the gap again, she said, 'It can't move now.'

She looked up at Flame, her face troubled, suddenly. 'I don't like to kill things,' she said.

 'Neither do I, Ash,' said Flame. 'But we really don't have any choice in this: you've seen what the screeglings have done to Mum and Dad.' She crouched down beside her sister, who shuffled to one side.

Ash pointed. 'It's just in there.'

'Thanks,' muttered Flame, as she peered between the rough floorboards. 'Yes, I can see its yellow eyes and I can smell it. Urgh!' She put her hand over her mouth and coughed violently. When it subsided, she took a deep breath and held it. Bringing her finger level with her face, she pointed her right index finger down towards the screegling. A split second later, her power of Fire burst out of her finger. Thin and precise as a laser, it hit the screegling. A loud hissing like a tyre losing air issued from the gap, followed by trail of acrid yellow smoke. Ash and Flame began to cough. As she waved away the smoke, Flame said, 'Heck, that smell is gross.'

'I think we'd better re-open the window,' said Marina, grabbing one of the casement handles and pushing it out. Instantly, cool air blew around the dusty attic.

'Now what?' said Ariel.

'We can't leave the screegling here,' said Flame,

getting up from the floor and brushing the dust from her jeans.

'I'll go and get some buckets,' said Ariel.

'Well, I'm not touching them,' said Marina.

'Nope, I didn't think you would,' said Ariel.

A few minutes later, Ariel came back with two black plastic buckets. The Sprite Sisters stared at one another, realising that they would now have to extract the dead screegling from the gap between the floorboards and put it in the bucket.

But Ariel was calm and matter of fact. She crouched down and pointed her finger at the incinerated screegling, using her power of Air. Without touching it, she lifted the foul thing up through the gap in the floorboards and dropped it into the bucket. The Sprite Sisters peered in.

'It is dead, isn't it?' said Marina.

'Looks dead to me,' said Flame.

'What does your magic stone say, Ash?' asked Marina.

Ash held up her stone beside the screegling: it neither lit up, nor beeped. 'We're safe,' she said, and peered into the bucket. 'It's bigger than I thought it would be. We won't fit many of them into the bucket.'

Marina shuddered. 'It's gross.'

'It's huge,' said Ariel, screwing up her nose.

'I wonder why Sidney says it's half-goblin?' said Ash.

'Perhaps because it has the intelligence of a goblin,' said Flame.

Ariel stared at the screegling. 'Look at its face,' she said, with a shudder. 'Its eyes are huge and bulbous.'

Marina turned away. 'I've had enough,' she said and walked to the window.

Ariel, Ash and Flame continued to stare at the dead screegling. Its body was black and shiny, its six legs were jointed and hairy

'It's the most disgusting thing I've ever seen,' whispered Ariel. 'And, look – it has fangs.'

Ash peered. 'Urgh, yes, you're right.'

Flame was silent, overwhelmed by revulsion and the sense that something really, really horrible was happening at Sprite Towers. And all the time, she kept wondering. Why are these disgusting creatures swarming through Sprite Towers?

'One down, but how many to go?' said Ash, standing up.

'Could be hundreds,' said Marina.

'Even *thousands*,' said Ariel. 'You saw the eyes on the lawn.'

Flame, Marina and Ash sighed. 'Ariel, do belt up,' they said together.

Chapter Fourteen
THE HUNT

The four sisters agreed to search the attics and work their way down through the house. Ash's stone would guide them to the parts of the house where the screeglings were hiding. The cupboards would be the most difficult places to search, and there were plenty of them at Sprite Towers. Once they knew a screegling was in the vicinity, Marina and Ash would use their magic power to establish exactly where it was hiding. Marina reasoned she could flush out any screeglings that were lurking in pipes by sending a blast of water through them. Ash would bind them, so they could not move. Flame now knew she could use her power of Fire to destroy them. Ariel would then lift the dead screegling into the bucket.

Then what did they do with them? Ash wanted to put the screeglings back into the earth, where they belonged. Contrarily, Ariel thought she could use her power of Air to send the screeglings into space, but admitted that their neighbours in the village might be startled and too many questions asked. Marina wanted to send them as far away as possible. Flame agreed with Ash and suggested that when they had 'de-screegled' the house, they take the screeglings back to the hole in the ground.

The first thing they had to do was find them. As soon as the magic stone beeped and glowed the sickly yellow that indicated the presence of screeglings, Marina and Ash set to, running their hands along the dusty attic walls and floorboards, using their magic power to sense what lay behind. Ariel used her pin-sharp hearing to detect the clicking that revealed their whereabouts. Every now and then, a telltale whiff of the screeglings' terrible smell would waft up and the Sprite Sisters knew there was one close by. As soon as they located a screegling, Ash bound it so that it could not move, then Flame used her power of Fire as a laser or Marina used her power of Water to send a needle of ice to pierce its carapace. Finally, Ariel used her power to lift it up and drop it into the bucket.

Apart from the screegling they had found earlier, they found another fifteen under the attic floorboards. Three were found right at the back of a huge, dark cupboard, which Ash and Flame dealt with. Two more were discovered in the pipe work, which they couldn't get to, so Marina flushed them away. When the space was 'screegle-free', Ariel used her power of Air to create fresh, fragrant air. As they used their magic, each of the sisters noticed how much stronger her power felt.

By the time the sisters got to the towers, they were tired, hungry and covered in dust. With a quick check of the towers – Ash's stone did not beep or glow – they were ready to go down. As they closed the door of the East Tower, the sisters were confident that this part of the house was now free of screeglings.

But the top of the house was not quite clear. One screegling remained unnoticed, having climbed its way outside. It sat, now, in the gutter of the East Tower, high in the air, its stench blown away by the wind, its clicking legs unheard, its yellow eyes watching Pudding on the lawn and a thin trail of slime dripping from its jaws.

Inside Sprite Towers, the sisters brushed off cobwebs from their clothes and made their way down the stairs to the second floor. There they washed their faces and hands in the bathroom then, descending the stairs to the first floor, they looked in on their parents. Ottalie and Colin were feeling much the same and Flame began to feel anxious that they had been so badly affected by the screeglings. Should she call the doctor, she wondered. What if their illness was nothing to do with screeglings and they needed medical attention?

But Flame's intuition told her that once the screeglings were out of the house, her parents would soon be better. There was no doubt that it helped the girls to have their parents out of the way at this time. What would happen if they saw the buckets of dead screeglings? Just a little longer, thought Flame, shutting the bedroom door. With an offer of fresh hot water bottles and cups of tea, and an assurance to their mother that they were happy to get their own supper, the four sisters trundled down the stairs with the buckets.

As they opened the kitchen door, the stench of live screeglings hit them in the face for the second time that day. They rushed to open the back door and windows, then Ash and Flame took the buckets outside the back door and hid them in some shrubs. Ash covered them with her binding magic, so that nothing could come in or out of the buckets. Flame used her power to protect them, to help keep them out of sight. 'We'll deal with these as soon as we get the house clear,' she said.

Inside, Marina had let Archie out of the utility room. He sniffed around the kitchen, growling, before she sent him outside. Then Flame and Marina pushed open the big sash windows in the dining room and drawing room, while Ash filled the kettle for the tea and bottles and Ariel looked for more buckets.

'I'm starving,' said Marina, coming back into the kitchen and opening the fridge.

'Mum said to heat up the fish pie that's in there,'

said Flame, coming up behind her. A minute later, the pie was warming in the Aga and some home-grown vegetables were cooking on the hob.

When everything was ready, the sisters took their food through to the dining room and sat at the huge polished wooden table, away from the stench of screeglings. After their fish pie, they ate bowls of homemade apple and blackberry crumble, covered with custard.

'That's better,' said Marina, rubbing her tummy. She pulled her mobile phone out of her pocket and flicked through the text messages, biting the side of her lip and giving a big sigh.

'You'll have time to do that later,' said Ash. 'We must press on while Mum and Dad are out of the way.'

'You don't want to go to sleep with any screeglings in your room,' said Ariel.

Marina shot Ariel withering look and drew in a sharp breath. Flame put out her hand. 'Don't start! We haven't time. Come on.'

'It'll be dark soon and then we can see the yellow eyes,' said Ash, picking up the plates from the table.

'Oh goodie, I can't wait,' said Marina, shoving her mobile back in her jeans pocket.

'Let's go and do the bedrooms,' said Flame. 'That way at least we'll be able to sleep without worrying about finding screeglings in our beds.'

Again that day, they climbed the staircase to the second floor of the house, which accommodated their four bedrooms and two bathrooms. They checked the airing cupboard where the linen and towels were kept and found two. They checked inside, behind, under and on top of every cupboard and in every drawer. Flame was unnerved to see two pairs of yellow eyes staring back at her from the corner of her wardrobe.

'How disgusting,' said Marina, beside her. 'Hurry up before they change shape and disappear.'

Flame shuddered at the thought of touching a screegling. It was bad enough to see their shiny black bodies and smell their revolting smell. 'Don't worry,' she said softly, as she focused on the two pairs of yellow eyes. 'They won't get away.' Quick as a flash, she raised her hand and her power of Fire shot from her finger. As the other screegling began to use its magic to shrink, she used her power on that one, too.

As swiftly as they could, the four Sprite Sisters worked together to clear the second floor. By the time they had finished, they had found twenty-three screeglings and filled three more buckets. Before they left that floor, the sisters created another Circle of Power to increase the magical protection and to stop the screeglings coming back. Then it was down the stairs to the first floor, which had their parents' bedroom, their grandmother's bedroom and sitting room, the big spare room and their bathrooms. Here they had to work silently. While Ottalie was unwell, she could still hear and the last thing the sisters wanted now was for their mother to start asking questions and stop them using their magic. They were in luck: Ottalie and Colin were sleeping so deeply that the sisters' work went unheard.

It was ten o'clock by the time the Sprite Sisters got to the ground floor of the house and they were now so tired they could hardly stand up. They had also run out of buckets, so emptied the dead screeglings at the back of the house, hidden in the shrubs.

Flame carried the buckets back into the house. 'I just hope Mum and Dad don't find the screeglings,' she said.

'I've bound them so that Archie and the foxes can't get to them,' said Ash.

Yawning, Ariel stumbled along behind. 'Do you suppose we could introduce a new word to the English language: to "de-screegle"?'

'Come on, let's "de-screegle" the drawing room,' said Flame. The big room, with its duck-egg-blue walls, cream sofas and carved fireplace, was everybody's favourite. Having found eight screeglings in there, the

162

girls moved through to the library and conservatory, where they found another nine screeglings, then the dining room, where they found eleven.

'I'm so sick of screeglings,' said Ariel, looking as if she might fall asleep where she was standing.

'Just the kitchen now,' said Flame, still focused and determined despite her fatigue.

'I need a drink,' said Ash.

'I need cake,' said Ariel, making for the pantry. A moment later she gave a short, sharp scream. Ash dashed into the pantry, pushed Ariel aside, held out her finger and bound the two screeglings that were beneath the shelf. Ariel stood gasping for breath. 'Sorry – the eyes made me jump,' she said, moving aside so that Flame could come in and use her power of Fire.

In the kitchen, Marina was busily using her power of Water to flush the screeglings that had earlier been in the pipes at the top of the house through the plumbing system and out into the drain. As they passed through, she used her power to send needles of ice to pierce the screeglings' carapaces. 'Two more down here,' she said, as her sisters came out of the pantry.

'And two in there,' said Flame. 'Let's have a rest.'

For the next five minutes, the Sprite Sisters drank apple juice and ate pieces of cake. 'Ah, that's better,' said Ariel.

Marina and Ash then used their powers to successfully locate the remaining screeglings in the kitchen – all fifteen of them. By the time they had been dealt with, the girls never wanted to look at nor smell another screegling in the whole of their lives.

As Ariel dragged herself across the kitchen to go up to bed, Flame said, 'Hang on a mo – we need to make the Circle of Power, to seal the protection around the house.'

With supreme effort, Ariel pushed her hair back from her face, stood up straight and helped her sisters to make a Circle of Power so strong that they were all nearly knocked over.

And with that, the four Sprite Sisters fell into their beds and slept until morning.

Chapter Fifteen
Thursday
ARE THEY GONE?

All through the night, the buckets and piles of dead screeglings lay hidden behind the shrubs at the back of the house. Before she went to bed, Flame had used her magic power to create a cloak of fire to protect them from curious nocturnal animals. Now, as she woke on Thursday morning, the screeglings were the first thing to enter her mind. We must get rid of them before Mum or Dad finds them, she thought, pulling herself up in bed. She pushed back her thick copper hair and stared across the room. Her whole body ached. She glanced at the clock on her bedside table: half seven. She sighed, still tired, and lay back against the pillow. Now is the time to think, to work out what is happening and why, she thought, drawing up the red duvet.

Flame liked the morning. It was her best time: her power of Fire, with its affinity to the direction of east on the compass, determined that. It was now, as she woke, that she could 'see' most clearly. She closed her eyes and for a few minutes used her gift of far-sightedness to explore the issues. Zak's face, with his hawk-like eyes, came straight into her mind. There was something fierce in his gaze. It was a gaze that challenged. Around him, Flame saw fire, noticed the boy's sardonic smile.

Ariel insists that Zak is connected to the screegling invasion, thought Flame. But how is he connected and why? If he is, then why has he come into our lives at this time and why has he used dark magic against us? Flame put these questions to the back of her mind, to let them wander and find their way though her consciousness. Often she did this, knowing that connections would be made and a pattern emerge. The answer would come. She just had to be patient and let her subconscious do the work. It was the one thing with which Flame Sprite could be patient.

She held up her long, slim hands and looked at them. My power of Fire is stronger and more refined, she thought. It has been an amazing feeling to use it again. I think my sisters would say the same about their powers. We have all got stronger. The battle against the screeglings was one of the most challenging things we have ever done with our magic. There were some scary moments and a few times when I did not think I could hold on to my power: but I did. We all did.

Could we have rid the house of the screeglings two years ago, I wonder? Glenda Glass was a different adversary in that we knew what she wanted. She wanted

Sprite Towers and she wanted to destroy our magic power. If our combined magic power has grown stronger since that time, have we attracted a new adversary with the power to match it? Like attracts like, they say: what you give out you get back. It is cause and effect. I may never have used my power of Fire if the screeglings had not invaded the house. Am I glad to have used it? I'm not sure … You never know your strengths and weakness until you are challenged: I am only fifteen, but I have learned that already.

For a while, Flame thought about Quinn and her friends. What would they say if they knew I had a magic power? Would they still speak to me? What names would they call me? I don't want to be different. But I *am* different. Unless I lose my power of Fire, I will always be different …

Then she began – as she always did when she woke – to plan her day. Naturally organised, the last thing Flame Sprite wanted was to waste time. The first thing we must do is to get rid of the dead screeglings, she decided. We must put them back into the hole that they sprang from and place the stone back on top. We must seal it with our magic so that it never moves again. Getting the screeglings back without being seen by Mum or Dad will be tricky. Dad may go to work at his office today, if he has a meeting. That would help – then one of us will need to distract Mum at the other side of the house.

The second thing, thought Flame, is Zak. We must talk about this strange boy and find out what we know about him. If it was Zak in the Wild Wood, what was he doing? If Ariel hadn't learned to fly and hadn't seen him or knocked the stone and released the screeglings, would Zak have found another way to confront us? Are there people outside the Sprite family who have magic powers? The only people I have met with magic power are other Sprites.

She smiled as she thought of Verena. She remembered her long-lost cousin, Charles Smythson, who had appeared at Sprite Towers two summers ago and was, at that time, under the influence of Glenda Glass's dark power. Charles had dark magic then, thought Flame, but he changed and he helped us. Is Zak a Sprite, another long-lost cousin? No, that didn't feel right somehow. Zak is somebody new, from outside the family.

So many questions and so few answers, she thought. But the answers will come. I will find them. I always do when I apply my mind to a problem.

The sound of a door shutting alerted Flame to her parents moving about downstairs. They must be feeling better this morning. Hauling her aching body out of bed, she walked through to the shower and checked on her sisters en route. They were all fast asleep. With the sudden need to check the dead screeglings, Flame showered and dressed as quickly as possible and went downstairs.

The aroma of coffee and toast wafted through the air as she opened the door into the kitchen. Colin and Ottalie were sitting at the table eating breakfast. Flame kissed them and asked how they were feeling. Much better, they said, and thanked her for helping out while they were unwell. They were pleased and relieved that the terrible smell seemed to have gone away. A mystery, her father described it. Flame smiled, unable to explain the truth of the screeglings. Nor was she now able to check them without alerting her parents. That would have to wait until after breakfast.

Flame poured herself a cup of coffee, made some more toast, scrambled two eggs and sat down to eat at the table. Her father, she learned, had a meeting this morning and would be off to his office in town. An architect, sometimes he worked at home and sometimes at his office. Her mother worked mostly at home, but this morning had a meeting with the music examining board. When Ottalie asked Flame if she would 'hold the fort' at the house, her daughter readily agreed, relieved that she and her sisters would not need to dodge about, secretly, holding buckets of dead screeglings. Her sisters, Flame said, were still fast asleep.

'You all seem to have been very tired recently and sleeping later and later in the mornings,' said Ottalie.

'It's because we're growing so fast,' said Flame, scooping up a forkful of egg.

'Or are worn out from staring at your mobile phones all day long,' said Dad.

'That just makes us cross-eyed.'

'You've developed a good line in grunts.'

'What, as a way of replying to questions?'

'Hm,' said Colin, in a doubtful tone. 'Hardly get a word out of you and Marina these days – you both just keep your noses pinned to your phones and grunt when I ask you something.'

'We're trying to conserve our energy, so that we grow properly,' said Flame, with a grin. Ottalie laughed.

Colin sighed. 'Daughters – who'd have 'em, eh.'

They ate in silence for a moment, then Colin said, 'At least that horrible smell has gone.'

'I wonder what it was?' said Ottalie.

Flame stayed silent.

'It's a complete mystery,' said Colin.

As soon as she finished her breakfast and cleared the plates, Flame ran upstairs to wake her sisters. 'Come on, come on,' she said, shaking each of them and opening their bedroom curtains. Marina and Ariel groaned, dozily. Ash sat up, immediately alert. Within half an hour, and a few minutes after Ottalie had left the house, the four Sprite Sisters were assembled in the kitchen. Flame made toast and cooked scrambled eggs for her sisters, then hurried them through their breakfast. Gradually Marina and Ariel came to.

After the storm the evening before, the air had cooled. There was thick dew on the grass and a faint whiff of autumn as the girls walked round to the bushes to find the buckets of dead screeglings. Now that their battle was over, they found it difficult to even look at them. Ash peered down at the buckets and screwed up her nose. 'Blimey, they are repellent,' she said. 'You know what they remind me of?'

'What?' said Ariel, standing beside her and screwing up her nose.

'Those beetles that come out at night and eat the slugs. Devil's Coach-Horse, they're called. They've got ferocious-looking jaws and they raise their tail end when they're alarmed.'

Ariel nodded. 'I know the ones you mean.'

'You're right,' said Flame. 'They do look a bit like them, but the screeglings are a lot bigger.'

'And Devil's Coach-Horse beetles don't have those weird yellow eyes,' said Ash.

Ariel shuddered. 'Look at the slime in this bucket – it's green.'

'Perhaps that's the goblin bit of them,' said Ash.

'It's gross,' said Ariel, turning away.

Marina put up her gloved hands. 'I'm not touching them. I'll come with you, but I – am – not – touching – them.'

'It's amazing what you can do when you have to,' said Flame, but Marina kept her hands raised. 'Okay, go and get a spade from the stable then, so we can make the hole big enough to get this lot down it,' said Flame.

Marina wandered off over the lawn, her mobile in hand, her face pressed close to it as she read her text messages.

Wearing thick gloves, Flame, Ash and Ariel picked up the buckets of dead screeglings and walked over the lawn towards the Wild Wood.

Ash looked up at the sky. 'The air feels cooler today.'

'Yes, and the trees have that heavy, late summer look,' said Flame.

'In another few weeks we'll be back at school.'

'With Zak,' said Ariel.

They stopped and turned as Marina called to them. 'Won't we need a ladder to get over the wall?'

Flame screwed up her face. 'Of course!' she said.

'The hole is on the track, the other side of the wall – I'd completely forgotten. Hang on, Marina!'

Ash laughed. 'We'll never get over a four-metre wall with a ladder – and we'd need another one the other side of the wall.'

Flame put down her buckets and looked around.

Marina walked up to them. 'What's the matter?' she asked.

'We won't be able to get over the wall with a ladder,' said Ash. 'It's too high.'

'We could walk down the driveway and around the outside of the wall to the place on the track,' said Flame.

'It's miles round – it'll take us ages,' said Marina. 'We don't know how long Mum will be.'

'And it means we'd have to leave the grounds,' said Flame. 'If someone came round, we wouldn't be here.'

'There's the little door in the wall – the one we used our magic power to open a couple of years ago, when we had to get rid of the monster slugs,' said Ash.

'It would still take us time to open that,' said Flame.

They were silent, each wondering what to do. Flame scratched her head. 'Oh dear,' she said, with a heavy sigh. 'We've got to get rid of this lot as quickly as possible.'

'Do they have to go back in the hole in the ground?' said Marina.

'I think they should,' said Ash.

'It makes sense,' agreed Flame. 'We can bind the hole so that no more screeglings will come out of it.'

They were silent again.

'I have an idea,' said Ariel, looking towards the Wild Wood.

'What?' said Ash.

'I could use my magic power to fly the buckets over.'

Flame laughed. 'And us, I suppose!'

Ariel turned to her eldest sister, her mouth a determined line across her small face. 'Well, yes, I probably could,' she said.

Marina laughed. 'What, like on the films, where the superhero takes hold of someone's hand and they both fly?'

'I don't see why not,' said Ariel. 'It's worth a try.'

'Well, let's do it then,' said Flame. 'There's no time to lose.'

'What, just like that? You're not going to argue?'

'No, I'm not going to argue,' said Flame. 'Come on!'

'You'd better bind the buckets again, Ash, so that nothing falls out,' said Marina. 'We don't want anyone to find bits of screeglings.'

They carried on over the lawn to the wall. There,

Ash set about using her magic power of Earth on the buckets of dead screeglings, then Ariel stepped forward. She was about to send over the first bucket when Flame said, 'Wait.' Ariel hesitated.

'We don't know if anyone is the other side of the wall,' said Flame. 'You'd better take me over first.'

'Really?'

'Yes, really – come on!' said Flame, her voice urgent now.

'But I need a moment to focus my mind,' said Ariel. 'It's different from just sending the buckets over.'

'Let's all think about our magic power for a moment,' said Ash, and they stood silent on the wet grass.

A minute later, Ariel was ready. She took hold of Flame's hand and called in her magic power of Air. And then, as if a wind had suddenly lifted them, the two sisters rose up. Ash and Marina watched, their faces bright with excitement, as Ariel and Flame flew over the high brick wall and disappeared the other side. Half a minute later, Ariel flew back and landed on the lawn beside Marina and Ash. Then, one by one, Ariel used her magic power to send the buckets of dead screeglings over the wall. Standing on the track the far side of the wall, Flame watched over them and shouted back to her sisters.

When all the buckets had been sent, Ariel took hold of Marina's hand and lifted her across the wall. A minute later, Marina and Flame stood together on the flinty track, laughing at their experience, and Ariel flew back to collect Ash. Once her three sisters were all on the track, Ariel flew back over the wall and found an empty bucket in the stables. On the lawn at the side of the house, lay a few dead screeglings. Using her magic power of Air, Ariel lifted them into the empty bucket. Once she was sure there were no more dead screeglings lying about, she picked up the bucket and carried it to the wall. As Ariel flew over the wall with the last bucket, Flame, Marina and Ash hunted in the brambles for the hole in the ground. Ariel flew back once more to collect the spade. Soon Ash found the hole in the ground.

'Don't touch the stone,' said Flame, looking down at the huge lump of flint.

Ash reached into her pocket and pulled out her magic stone. Lying on the flat of her palm, the round, brown stone began to glow. 'It's the same yukky colour as it was with the screeglings,' she said. 'I agree we shouldn't touch anything.'

They waited for Ariel to arrive, so that she could lift the stone with her power of Air.

She stepped forward and pointed her finger and a moment later the knobbly flint shifted sideways to reveal a tunnel running down into the earth.

'It's too narrow to get all the dead screeglings in there easily,' said Ariel.

'I don't think we should use the spade to widen it,' said Flame.

'I've just gone to get it!' said Ariel, with a groan.

'I know, but the soil may be tainted with dark magic.'

'I can widen the tunnel,' said Ash, and she set about using her magic power to increase the size of the hole. Once that was done, Ariel used her power to lift the screeglings, one by one, out of the buckets and into the hole. Ash bound them in, Ariel moved the stone back to cover the hole – and they were done.

'Thank heavens for that,' said Marina.

'We'd better make a Circle of Power around it,' said Flame. 'Let's be quick – someone might see us.'

'If they haven't already,' said Ash.

The four sisters moved into a circle, took hold of each other's hands and made the fastest Circle of Power that they had ever done. With that, Ariel lifted her sisters, the buckets, the spade and herself back into the grounds of Sprite Towers.

As the sun broke through the clouds, the Sprite Sisters walked back over the lawn towards the house. Their faces registered relief and satisfaction. 'That was truly amazing,' said Marina and the others laughed.

'Let's hope it's the last we'll see of the screeglings,' said Flame.

'That may depend on Zak,' said Ariel. She glanced at Marina and saw her face tense.

'You must be exhausted, Ariel,' said Ash.

Ariel laughed. 'I'm not sure I have any more magic power left in me!'

'A piece of Mum's fruitcake will soon put that right,' said Ash, and they laughed again.

Up on the gutter around the East Tower, the lone screegling that had eluded the Sprite Sisters' magic power the day before focused its big yellow eyes on the four girls walking over the grass. Gorged on a diet of worms and insects that it had found in the gutters, the shiny black screegling was growing bigger and bigger. In the last day it had wandered all over the roof of Sprite Towers, leaving a trail of vile dribble, its foul smell carried away by the wind. Once or twice a crow had come down to try to eat it, but had flown away as soon as it smelled the screegling. Not even the crows could put up with the stench. As the Sprite Sisters opened the back door and walked into the kitchen, the shiny black screegling opened its huge jaws and tore at a worm.

Chapter Sixteen
THE MATTER OF ZAK

The easy mood the sisters had shared that morning was soon interrupted by the ringing and beeping of mobile phones. As they sat at the kitchen table eating fruitcake and drinking apple juice, Flame and Marina's attention was on their phone chatter, while Ash and Ariel looked on in bemused silence.

'Quinn wants to know if he and Zak can come and play tennis tomorrow,' Flame said to Marina. 'Friday, it'll be, won't it?'

Marina nodded. 'Mm, I've had a text from Zak about it.'

'We need to talk about it before we decide,' said Flame.

'So soon?' said Ash. 'You only played tennis with Zak and Quinn a few days ago.'

'Hang on a minute,' said Ariel, trying to swallow a mouthful of cake. 'Do we want Zak here again?'

'It seems daft, given what he may have done,' said Ash. Marina's face clouded. Ash looked at her and said, 'I know you like him, but this is really important.'

'We need to get to the bottom of the screegling mystery,' said Flame. As her phone beeped again, she groaned and picked it up. 'Let's turn them off for a mo, Marina,' she said, pressing various buttons and putting the phone on the table. Marina did the same, with some reluctance, then they all sat waiting as if no one knew where to start.

Ariel sat up. 'I can only repeat what Sidney told me. He warned us to be careful of "the boy with hawk-like eyes". Since we don't know anybody apart from Zak who fits that description, I think we can assume Sidney means him. Do you agree?'

'You could ask Sidney,' said Flame.

'Yep, I will do when we've finished,' said Ariel. She drew a big breath and continued, 'There are two other things I haven't told you.'

'I hate it when you say that,' said Marina. 'Please, no more vile insect things.'

Flame's face tensed. 'What are they?'

'The first thing is that Zak twice asked me if I think about flying,' said Ariel.

'*What?*'

Marina started. 'Maybe he meant in a plane?'

Ariel shook her head. 'No – I asked him that. He said, "up in the air like a bird".'

Flame blinked in surprise. Marina's mouth dropped open.

'The first time he asked me got me thinking about

it, I admit,' said Ariel. 'I'd been wondering if it were possible, but after he talked about it I began to see it as something real.'

Flame's face darkened. 'Do you think he knew you would think about it?'

Ariel shook her head again. 'I don't know, but it's an odd thing to ask someone. Then, on Friday night, I flew over Sprite Towers for the first time. It was when I fell and hit the stone. You were all away, remember?' Her sisters nodded. 'So on Saturday, we were sitting on the terrace after you'd finished playing tennis. That was the second time Zak asked me. While you were all chattering, he turned to me and said very quietly, "Well, have you thought about it?" I had this feeling he was *expecting* me to fly!'

'How strange,' said Flame.

'It's a strange thing to ask someone once, let alone twice,' said Marina.

'Especially someone you've only just met,' added Ash.

'It was really weird,' said Ariel.

'What did you say?' asked Flame.

Ariel shrugged. 'I didn't know what to say and I knew I was blushing. I could feel Zak's eyes boring into me and I felt that, somehow, he must know my secret. I ran into the house to the cloakroom, then I went up to my room.'

'I came and sat on your bed and asked you what Zak had said to make you dash off,' said Ash. 'And you told me, but at that point I didn't understand the full significance.'

They all looked at Ariel. 'How could Zak have possibly known that I was trying to fly – *have flown* – unless he'd seen me?' she said. 'Both times, he asked me in a quiet voice, as if this was something secret between us.'

'Perhaps he can read minds,' said Flame.

Ariel nodded. 'I wondered about that. Ash and I both feel he looks right through us, as if he can see what we're thinking. Don't we, Ash?"

Ash nodded. 'He makes me feel very exposed.'

Ariel sat forward. 'Don't you see – it must have been Zak in the Wild Wood!'

Flame drew herself up and placed her hands on the table as if she were chairing a meeting. 'Okay, I think we should assume – for the moment – that Zak is connected to the screeglings.'

'And that he has some kind of magic power,' said Ariel.

'And that he is not as he seems,' said Ash.

'Which is what?' asked Marina, looking flustered.

'Well – he *seems* friendly,' said Ash. 'But I don't

think we found the screeglings a heap of fun.'

'Look how ill they made Mum and Dad,' said Ariel.

Flame rubbed her hands across her face. 'But, *why?* Here's a boy who's new to us, is new to Drsydale's, where he'll be studying with us in a few weeks' time. It just doesn't make any sense. What have we done to draw him to us? You know how Mrs Duggery always said that what you give out you get back? That we draw things to us.'

Ash smiled. 'Grandma tells us that, too.'

'Yes, she does.'

Marina shook her head. 'I don't know what to think.'

'You like Zak and he's confused you,' said Ash.

'I do like him.'

'But do you trust him?'

Marina thought about this, then said, 'I know what you mean about him looking through you.'

'Do you trust him?' repeated Ash.

Marina shook her head again. 'No – I'm not sure. Not really … I feel drawn in, but …'

'I'm sure Sidney is warning us for our best interests and that we should be careful of Zak,' said Flame.

'But should we invite him here again?' asked Ash.

'If he wants to get to Sprite Towers, he'll walk through the Wild Wood at night. We can't stop him doing that. I think we need to confront him. He needs to understand that we've defeated the screeglings. There are questions he needs to answer.'

'Such as, why did you try to poison us?' said Ariel.

'And, can you fly?' said Ash.

'And what do you know about screeglings?' said Ariel.

Ash looked at Flame. 'How will we get Zak on our own, without Quinn?'

'I can get Quinn away, but I'd like to ask Zak some questions, too,' said Flame, her face thoughtful. She looked at Marina. 'Could you get Quinn away for a while – take him to see something?'

Marina shrugged. 'It may look a bit odd, but yes, I s'pose so.'

'It would be better if we confronted Zak,' said Flame.

'You're treating me like I'm stupid!' said Marina, her face flushing.

'No, I'm not! I just think we'll be more detached,' said Flame. 'That's all.' She looked round at Marina, who sat back in her chair, her arms folded across her chest. 'What do you know about him so far?'

Marina ran her fingers through her dark curly hair as she thought about this. 'He's nearly sixteen. He's an only child. His parents have just moved here. I think he said his father is a businessman and his mother is a lawyer.'

'And he's boarding at Drysdale's?' asked Ash.

'Yes,' said Marina.

'When is Zak's birthday?' asked Ash.

'I think he said the middle of November,' said Marina.

'So he's a Scorpio,' said Flame. 'Deep, secretive and has a sting in his tail.'

'What is he interested in?' said Ash.

'He likes reading – he seems quite deep,' said Marina. 'He says he thinks about stuff.'

'He didn't ask you about flying?' said Ariel.

Marina shook her head again. 'Nope.'

They were silent for a moment. Ariel put her chin on her hands and said, 'Do you think – do you think that there are other people with magic powers in the world, apart from the Sprite family?'

Flame laughed. 'There must be! We're not likely to be the only ones with magic power.'

Marina and Ash smiled. 'What do you think?' Ariel asked them.

'It would be a bit weird if the Sprites were the only people in the whole world to have magic power,' said Ash. 'It would be like saying that Earth is the only planet with life on it, in the whole of the Universe.'

'And you, Marina?' asked Ariel.

Marina nodded. 'I agree with Flame and Ash.'

Ariel sat back. 'But that means … that means we could always be using our magic powers when we're grown up. It means that other people with magic power might set out to get us and we might have lots of battles ahead of us.' She looked round at her sisters, her grey eyes wide. 'We might have very busy lives.'

'Yes, I suppose we might,' said Flame.

Ariel looked at her. 'Do you think Sidney is trying to warn us about something bigger – something outside the Sprite family?'

Flame hesitated. 'He may be.'

Marina and Ash gazed at their little sister. Not for the first time, she surprised them with her insight.

'I don't understand why Zak would want to hurt us,' said Marina.

'Maybe he likes to play games,' said Flame. 'Maybe he's testing us.'

'Perhaps he's under a curse,' said Marina. 'You know – like he doesn't have any choice.'

'That's possible,' said Flame.

'You'd like that, 'cos then you could save him,' said Ariel, with a wry smile. 'Saint Marina, Saviour of Cursed Boys.'

'Ha blooming ha,' said Marina, making a face at her

little sister. 'But how would he know we have magic powers? Nobody knows – we keep it secret.'

Flame looked thoughtful. 'Mrs Duggery always said that people with magic power recognise other people who have magic power.'

'So why don't we recognise Zak, if he has power?' said Ash.

'Probably because we've not been tuned in to our power for a long while,' said Ariel.

Ash leaned forward. 'Ariel, you haven't told them the second thing about Zak.'

'Now what?' said Flame.

Ash looked at Ariel.

'Oh yes – the yellow eyes,' said Ariel. 'Well, after we had that crazy bicycle race on Tuesday, we sat under the copper beech tree and had tea.'

'Yes,' said Flame.

'And?' said Marina.

Ariel took a deep breath. Everybody waited. Then she burst out, 'While we were sitting at the table, Zak looked round at me.'

'And?' said Marina.

'And his eyes were yellow – just like the screeglings.'

Marina looked as if something had kicked her in the gut. Flame frowned and looked away.

They were silent for what felt a long while. Then Marina said, 'It could have been a trick of the light.'

'Yes,' agreed Flame. 'But it might not have been.'

'Do you think Zak is a screegling, too?' said Ariel. 'Maybe he turns into one at night.'

'Stop it!' said Marina.

'I was only wondering,' said Ariel. 'I've never seen a person with yellow eyes before.'

They were silent again then Flame said, 'Well, I think we need to find out what makes Zak tick.'

'I think we should confront him,' said Ariel.

'Yes, but what would we *say*?' said Marina. 'If it's not him who sent the screeglings, he'll think we're mad and he'll learn we've got magic powers, right?'

They all looked at Marina. She continued, 'And, as Ash says, if it *is* him, he's not likely to admit it. He'll know about us and we still won't know about him. In which case, we're left looking like right lemons. Sidney didn't say, "Zak sent the screeglings". He said, "Beware of the boy with hawk-like eyes". That could mean anything. It doesn't mean it was Zak in the Wild Wood. It doesn't necessarily mean he sent the screeglings. If you charge up and confront him, we could end up looking completely daft. Look how cool Zak is – he watches and he listens and he thinks before he speaks.'

'He doesn't give much away, for sure,' said Flame.

Ash put her chin in her hands and stared across the kitchen. 'He's not likely to pour his heart out and say, "Oh yes it was me all along, I'm so sorry"!'

Flame bit her lip and crossed her long arms over her chest. 'Oh dear,' she said. She looked at Ariel. 'Why don't you ask Sidney.'

'What am I asking?' said Ariel, getting up from her chair.

'Well – what does, "Beware of the boy with hawk-like eyes" specifically mean?' said Flame.

'Was Zak responsible for the screeglings?' said Marina. 'Has he got magic power?'

'Was it him in the Wild Wood?' said Ash, also getting up.

'Is he a good person?' said Marina.

While Ash and Ariel went through to the hallway, Flame and Marina settled back into social chit-chat. A few minutes later, Ariel and Ash re-appeared, their faces drawn.

'What did he say?' asked Flame and Marina together, as the younger girls sat down again at the table.

'Not a lot,' said Ariel, giving a frustrated sigh and leaning on her elbows.

'What do you mean?' said Flame.

'He did what Mrs Duggery used to do,' said Ash.

'What – told you to go and find out for yourself?' said Marina.

Ariel sighed again.

'It's just like Mrs Duggery,' said Ash. 'Just when we needed her, she would tell us we had to be self-reliant. Remember?'

'Yes,' said Flame. 'She let us find our own way out of the portal, remember that?' Her sisters smiled, recalling one of their previous adventures.

'Well, Sidney's doing the same,' said Ash.

Suddenly feeling the weight of responsibility as the eldest, Flame felt she needed to explain this. 'I think what Sidney and Mrs Duggery mean is that if someone is always there for you to lean on when you need them, you never learn to do things for yourself.'

'Ariel said that's what Sidney told her,' said Ash.

'He went silent,' said Ariel. 'He's never done that before. I mean, for heaven's sakes, we've just had the house invaded by the most disgusting things you could imagine ...'

'And we only just got rid of them,' added Ash.

'Did Sidney say anything that was helpful?' asked Marina.

'He repeated what he'd told me before,' said Ariel. 'Beware of the boy with hawk-like eyes.'

'And then he was silent?'

Ariel nodded. 'I've never heard Sidney quiet. Usually I can't stop him talking.'

They sat in silence, their faces thoughtful. Eventually Ariel yawned. 'I'm so tired after yesterday and my whole body aches,' she said and flopped her head onto the table.

'Me too,' said Marina, lowering her head on her arms.

The silence was broken by Ash. 'What would happen, do you think, if we said nothing to Zak?'

Flame looked at her. 'What – act as if nothing has happened? Hm, interesting idea.'

Ariel sat bolt upright. 'But surely that would be letting him get away with it?'

'If we acted normally, it would show him how strong our magic is – that we've beaten him and we're not fazed by his magic,' said Flame, pulling her hair back. 'It might be more subtle, perhaps more strategic.'

'It could save us a lot of potential embarrassment,' said Marina.

Ariel looked outraged. 'But we can't let him off the hook!'

'I didn't mean that,' said Ash. 'I just meant that perhaps we ought not to rush this.'

'Humph.'

'We wouldn't be "letting him off the hook",' said Flame. 'We'd be biding our time. I think Marina's right – Zak is not going to open up. He won't say, "I went to a magic class and thought I'd practise on you lot, ha ha".' She looked round at her sisters. 'I have a strong feeling there's much more to Zak than we know at the moment, but I don't think we'll get anywhere if we confront him right now. I think we ought to wait and watch.'

'But you hate waiting,' said Ariel.

'I do,' agreed Flame. 'And I also hate not knowing, but I don't think we have a lot of choice at the moment.' She looked round at her sisters again. 'At least I've realised my magic is still a part of me and that I can't run away from it.'

'Nor us,' said Ariel.

'Nor you – much as I want to at times,' said Flame. Ariel laughed.

'What about you, Marina?' asked Ash. 'How do you feel about your magic power now?' They looked at their dark-haired sister. She looked down at the table, at first avoiding their gaze, then summoning the confidence to look back at them, one by one. 'I accept that I have the responsibility of having a magic power,' she said. 'It's not exactly easy, as a teenager, with hormones roaring round my body, but I expect I shall cope.'

'And what about Zak?' asked Flame.

'I will be careful. We must all be on our guard.'

'See if you can find out anything more about him,' said Ash.

Ariel looked at Marina. 'Are you sure you know whose side you are on?'

'Yes, of course – I don't want the screeglings back any more than you do.'

'If it was a choice between us or Zak, who would you choose?'

Marina stared at Ariel. 'Well you, of course – my family! But it would never come to that.'

Ariel shrugged. 'Sidney said to beware.'

'I will be careful, I promise, and I will try to find out more about Zak.'

'Well, take great care and don't leave yourself open to his magic,' said Flame. Marina nodded, acknowledging this advice.

'Zak must have magic or Sidney wouldn't have said beware,' said Ariel. 'I still think we should confront him.'

'That's probably what he's expecting,' said Flame.

Ash shook her head. 'We'd expose ourselves too much. Let's wait and see what happens. We need to be able to tie Zak to something specific and at the moment it's all too vague.'

'The screeglings weren't vague,' said Ariel. Marina shivered at the thought of them.

'So, will you play tennis with Quinn and Zak tomorrow?' said Ash.

'We need to get Zak here to be able to talk to him,'

said Flame. 'I think so, though I don't like the idea of him being here.'

'Nor me, but it will give us the chance to look at him in a new light,' said Ash.

'This time we'll be ready,' said Ariel.

Five minutes later, Ash and Ariel went off down the garden with Archie to feed and water the rabbits and guinea pigs. Flame and Marina went up to their rooms. When Ottalie returned a little while later, she would have no idea that her older daughters and her younger daughters had communicated with each other. By lunchtime they had settled back into their usual bickering, and even Ottalie's patience was stretched by the constant beeping of the mobiles.

With all traces of the screeglings apparently removed, the Sprite Sisters used the afternoon to rest and recoup their energy. As she lay on her bed reading, Flame found it difficult to relax. Something was gnawing at the back of her mind.

I have a sense that there is more to come, she thought. I must warn Marina to be *really* careful. Ash and Ariel will be, but will Marina let her heart rule her head? I know she says she'll be on her guard with Zak, but I wonder if she will be able to see him clearly.

Chapter Seventeen
Friday
MIND GAMES

Flame did not intend to get angry. She intended to be cool and aloof, to watch Zak with seeming disinterest and to quietly assess him. But Flame Sprite was not wired for non-reaction. One spark and her temper could explode – particularly on a hot day, which this was, now that the storm had passed The moment Zak and Quinn cycled up the driveway, she was on red alert, could feel her pulse quicken as the sense of outrage about the screegling invasion bubbled up inside her. Despite that, Flame had good manners and her greeting to the boys was polite and welcoming.

Quinn was, as always, charming and pleased to see her. The sisters were all pleased to see him. With Zak, however, things were complicated. Marina, Ash and Ariel felt the same as Flame and, like her, drew on their good manners to greet him. They watched him closely; Zak watched them with his hawk-like eyes and smiled as if nothing were amiss.

Zak was so seemingly relaxed that for one moment Flame thought they must have got it all wrong. Perhaps

Sidney Sprite meant someone else, she thought – but instinct told her to be wary of this boy, and Flame's instinct was rarely wrong. The very fact that Zak dared to be so relaxed annoyed her – and once Flame was annoyed that was it.

Marina looked at Zak with nervous eyes, unsure whether to smile or whether to shout at him for what he had done to them. She felt angry and hurt and wanted to show it, yet felt drawn to him. And she must be careful, that she knew.

Beside her, Ariel's eyes narrowed as she observed Zak and she wished she could march up and shout at him. How dare he act as if nothing has happened, she thought. Ash stood to the side, watching and listening, making sure she had weighed things up before she made a decision. But now Flame was walking with a bold step towards the tennis court and they were all following over the lawn. 'Let's have a change from mixed doubles,' she said.

'Shall we play singles instead?' asked Quinn, beside her. He looked round at Ash and Ariel, his dark eyes twinkling. 'We have spectators today.'

Ariel giggled, smitten as she was with Quinn. Ash smiled her calm smile.

'I thought maybe Marina and I could play you and Zak today,' said Flame.

Quinn stopped, screwed up his handsome face, and looked at her. 'Two girls against two boys? It's hardly fair. We're much stronger than you. We'll flatten you.'

'I wouldn't be so sure,' said Flame, with a dazzling smile. Quinn looked at her in awe. Zak stared out over the lawn, as if only half listening to the conversation. Marina glanced at Flame, thrown by her new strategy, but Flame caught her eye and gave her a knowing smile. Marina's heart leapt. 'Yes,' she said. 'I think that's a very good idea.'

Quinn looked at Marina and nodded. 'Okay by me, if that's the way you want to play. What do you think Zak?'

Zak turned to Flame and looked her in the eye, then Marina. 'We accept your challenge,' he said, with a smile.

'Good,' said Flame, taking in a deep breath and walking forwards again.

'This should be interesting,' Ariel whispered to Ash, as they followed.

'Flame's angry,' said Ash.

'I know.'

'I hope she can keep her temper.'

'I doubt Zak will notice if she does – he's so relaxed, he's almost horizontal,' whispered Ariel.

A few minutes later and they were ready to begin

play. The girls won the toss. Tall and athletic, with her copper hair tied up in a ponytail, Flame stretched high to serve and hit the ball across the net with such strength – perhaps even ferocity – that Quinn blinked with surprise and missed the shot.

'Ace,' he said, turning his racquet in his hand.

'Fifteen love,' called Ash, umpiring from a seat by the net at the side of the court.

'Well done, Flame,' whispered Ariel from the wooden bench.

The girls changed sides. Flame threw the ball high in the air to serve to Zak, then brought her racquet down on it with a power she had never felt before. Another ace. With four shots, Flame won the first game.

At the other end of the court, Quinn and Zak bristled, and when Quinn served it was with similar power. One game all. Then it was Marina's turn to serve. She wore a sports cap and also had her hair pulled up into a ponytail. Tennis was one of Marina's passions and today she let rip, serving with speed and agility. Within another few shots, the game was hers. Soon the boys realised the girls were playing with such determination that they'd better up their game. By the end of the second set, they were equal with one set each. Hot now, they stopped for five minutes to drink glasses of homemade lemonade, which Ottalie had brought out on a tray.

'Well,' said Quinn, wiping his forehead on his towel. 'What's got into you two?'

Flame and Marina smiled. 'Never underestimate the Sprite Sisters,' said Marina and she looked at Zak. He smiled back his cool smile. Quinn laughed.

Then it was back to the third set. Refreshed by the lemonade, the four players got into position and it was Flame's turn to serve. Tension crackled through the sticky August heat. The players' faces were taut now, both sides absolutely determined to win.

'How exciting,' said Ottalie, sitting on the bench beside Ariel. She loved to watch her daughters excel and her face glowed with pride as Flame and Marina won the first point in the game. By the time Colin joined them, halfway through the third set, the spectators were biting their nails. He squashed onto the bench beside his wife and daughter. 'Girls playing the boys – that's interesting,' he whispered. 'How are they doing?'

'Remarkably well,' whispered Ottalie.

'What's the score?'

'Third set; four games to the girls – three to the boys, Zak's serve.'

Colin nodded. 'Impressive,' he whispered, as Zak put a top-spin on his serve to Marina, which she did not manage to return well. 'Who's your money on?'

Ottalie shook her head. 'It's so close, it could go either way.'

'Flame and Marina,' whispered Ariel, looking up at her father 'I know they'll win.'

'How do you know?' whispered her father, with one eye on the rally they were now playing.

'I just know,' said Ariel. Colin looked askance at his youngest daughter. 'Well, it'll be close, whichever way it goes,' he whispered.

'Sssh,' said Ash.

The tension mounted as the two sides matched each other point for point in the next two games. Flame and Marina, Quinn and Zak tore around the court, bashing the tennis ball this way and that way – lobs, volleys, smashes, forehands, backhands – they played them all. Colin and Ottalie, Ash and Ariel held their breath as they got to five games all. Whoever won the next game would win the match. It was Marina to serve.

Ottalie put her hand over her mouth – she could hardly bear to watch. Colin rubbed his chin. Ariel clutched the bench. Ash drew in a long, deep breath. Each time Marina won her serve, she dropped the next point: fifteen love, fifteen all, thirty fifteen, thirty all, forty thirty, deuce. Two more points and she could win the match – and beat Zak.

Tired now, Marina summoned all her energy and focused her mind. Two more serves; two more points to win the match. Facing her across the court, Quinn waited. Marina threw the ball high and drove it hard to the far corner. But Quinn was quick and returned the serve with a strong forehand drive. Back and forth, back and forth the ball went. Colin and Ottalie, Ash and Ariel held their breath. Then, standing at the net, Flame tucked a volley right beneath her and the ball bounced off sideways on the boys' side of the court.

'Advantage Flame and Marina,' called Ash.

One more point. Marina and Flame changed sides. At the other end of the court, Zak waited, relaxed and cool, his sharp eyes waiting for the ball. As soon as Marina had hit the serve, she ran to the net beside Flame. Zak returned the shot over their heads, with a strong forearm drive. Marina jumped and caught the ball – and smashed it back, straight through the middle of the two boys.

The Sprite Sisters had won!

Quinn and Zak shook hands and smiled at one another in disbelief.

Flame and Marina did a high five, their faces wide with delight.

Colin and Ottalie stood up and clapped. 'Well played, all of you – fantastic match!' they called out.

Ariel and Ash jumped up and ran to their sisters. 'That was amazing!' said Ash. 'Epic!' said Ariel.

'Blimey, that was close,' said Flame, wiping her forehead.

'But you did it – I knew you would,' said Ariel, looking up at her sister with pride.

'Thank you for your faith in us,' said Flame, with a smile. Quinn came up to her and put his arm around her shoulder and they laughed together. Zak and Marina smiled at one another. 'Good game,' he said. 'Well played.'

'You, too,' she said with a big smile and for the moment, all anger was forgotten.

Ash let down the net whilst Flame, Quinn, Zak and Marina collected the tennis balls.

'Let's all go up to the house and have a cup of tea,' said Ottalie, gathering the empty glasses.

'Okay,' they called to her.

'And cake,' said Ariel, picking up the jug.

'Yes, we can have cake,' said Ottalie. 'You do like cake, don't you.'

Ariel nodded. 'Cake is the way ahead.'

'You say some funny things,' said Ottalie with a smile.

'But it's true. Good cake is one of life's great pleasures.'

Ottalie laughed. 'That's the sort of thing people say when they're forty!'

'Well, I'm a very mature eleven-year-old,' said Ariel.

'Come on then, let's go and get some cake,' said Ottalie. Colin picked up the tray and together they walked to the house.

Later the Sprite family, Quinn and Zak relaxed on the terrace, drinking tea and eating cake. As they chatted, the sky darkened and from a distance came a deep rumble of thunder.

'What changeable weather we're having,' said Colin, looking up at the lowering sky. 'Hot and sticky one minute and stormy the next.'

'That's August for you,' said Ottalie.

Flame shivered and drew her sweater around her shoulders. She glanced over at Zak and Marina, who sat together at the far end of the table; Zak was talking and Flame noticed that her sister was watching him with guarded eyes. She turned to talk again to Quinn, but twice Flame noticed, out of the corner of her eye, that Zak looked up to the roof of the house as if he was looking for something. His eyes seemed to run along the length of the roof and back. Both times, he then looked at Flame and held her gaze for a second. Immediately

Flame looked up at the roof. What's up there, she wondered. There's something up there and Zak wants me to know …

Sensitive to Zak's words and movements, the other three Sprite Sisters picked up on this exchange. Marina, Ash and Ariel looked at Flame, then Zak, then up to the roof. Is he warning us about something, wondered Ash. What could it be, wondered Ariel. I'm sure there's good in him, thought Marina, wanting so much to trust this boy.

As thunder rumbled, they finished tea and cleared the table. Colin, Flame and Quinn carried the plates and glasses into the house. Ottalie picked up the teapot and followed them into the kitchen. Ash and Ariel watched as Marina and Zak walked off over the lawn.

'Shall I go with them?' said Ariel.

'I don't know,' said Ash.

'I hope she's on her guard. Did you notice that Zak looked up at the roof?

'Yes,' said Ash, with a thoughtful face.

'We'd better tell Flame that Marina's on her own,' said Ariel. 'I've got a funny feeling about it.'

They went into the house and found Flame in the hallway, coming out of the cloakroom. When they told their older sister that Marina was alone with Zak, she looked worried. 'Go and join them,' she said.

'Alright,' said Ash.

'Did you notice that Zak kept looking up at the roof?' asked Ariel.

Flame nodded.

'And then he looked straight at you,' said Ariel.

'Yes – I think he wanted me to see he was looking up there.'

'He looked up three times – one time you were talking to Quinn,' said Ash.

'I saw him, too, but what's on the roof that's of interest to Zak?' said Ariel.

'I don't know,' said Flame.

'Perhaps there's another screegling,' said Ariel.

'Maybe – but we can't look now,' said Flame, with a sinking feeling.

As Ash and Ariel went out of the front door, Flame stood still and looked around. Through the kitchen door came sounds of chatter and movement, but the big hallway was silent and she was alone. She walked over the chequered black and white tiles to the portrait of Sidney Sprite. As the storm grew closer, the light in the hallway darkened. Flame looked into her great-great-grandfather's eyes.

'Sidney, help me, please,' she whispered. 'What is

there about the roof that's of interest to Zak? Is there something up there or is he just thinking about flying, as Ariel mentioned? Oh Sidney, I wish you would talk to me …'

Flame started. Did Sidney just smile? It was the smallest of movements, a crinkle in the corner of his eyes, a tiny flicker at the side of his mouth. She blinked. Sidney's face gazed out, immobile, from the wall. Flame looked away, then looked back quickly, as if to catch him out.

No, she thought, it must have been a trick of the light. But Flame, with her analytical mind, questioned why Sidney might have smiled, if indeed he did, at that particular moment.

What was I thinking about at that moment? She considered this, backtracking on her thoughts. I was thinking that when something happens three times, it's not a coincidence. There's something on the roof that Zak wants us to know about.

Flame looked into the eyes of her great-great grandfather. 'That's what you want me to understand, isn't it,' she whispered. 'You want me to make that connection.'

Sidney's smiling face stared back her. Flame stepped back from the wall with a sudden sense of certainty. This is not over, she thought. We thought it was over – and it's not. There is something on the roof – and Zak knows about it.

With that, she opened the front door and ran to find Marina.

Chapter Eighteen
MARINA GOES WONKY

Thunder rumbled and the rain beat down as the Sprite family got ready for supper on Friday evening. Inside the kitchen everything was cosy and warm. The delicious aroma of slow-cooked lamb, herbs, onions and tomatoes wafted through the air. Pudding was curled up on the Windsor chair beside the Aga. Archie was lying on his mat in the corner of the kitchen. Ottalie was putting the final touches to her casserole. Colin was mashing potatoes and carrots into a puree with some butter, salt and black pepper.

'It sounds like the clouds are bashing against one another,' Ariel said to Ash, as they laid the table.

'They're arguing.'

'When are we going to camp out again in the caravan?'

'Not until the rain stops,' said Ash, lighting the candles in the middle of the long oak table.

Ariel screwed up her nose. 'No, it's not very nice out there at the moment.'

They looked round as Flame and Marina came into the kitchen.

A few minutes later they were all sitting down.

Mum served the casserole onto plates with a big ladle. Flame handed round the dishes of vegetables. Colin poured himself and Ottalie glasses of red wine.

'Yum,' said Ariel, as they all tucked in.

'Delicious,' said Flame. 'Thanks, Mum and Dad.'

For the next ten minutes they talked about the tennis match and what a good game both sides had played.

Marina listened and smiled, but said little. She ate slowly, as if in a dream.

'Sweetie, are you feeling okay?' asked her sharp-eyed mother. 'You're very quiet this evening.'

Marina smiled – but it was a bleary smile.

'You look as if you're not quite here,' said Ottalie.

'I'm okay, Mum, thanks,' said Marina. 'Bit tired, that's all.'

Her mother made a face that suggested she was not convinced.

'I should think you're worn out after that marathon match,' said her father, giving Marina a kind smile.

Marina laughed. 'Yep, it was amazing. I didn't know if we'd win.'

'We were on the edge of our seats,' said Ottalie.

'You did well to get those match points under such pressure,' said Colin.

'Changing the subject, will Grandma be home tomorrow?' said Ash.

'Yes, should be – unless Susan needs her help for one more day, in which case she'll be back on Sunday,' said Ottalie. She looked across at Flame. 'If Grandma doesn't come back tomorrow, we'll need you to be here on Saturday night, please. Your father and I have to go to the McFarlanes' party.'

'Okay,' said Flame.

'Oh Archie, you'll soon have your little friend Bert home again!' said Ariel, looking across at the black Labrador on his mat. Archie thumped his tail. 'Look – he's smiling,' said Ariel.

'Dogs don't smile,' said Flame.

'Yes they do – well, Archie does.'

'I agree with Ariel,' said Colin. 'You can tell whether a dog's happy or not, just like a human.'

'We don't wag tails,' said Flame.

'I meant by looking at their faces,' said Colin, with a chuckle.

The conversation bowled along, but, in between the talking and eating, Flame, Ash and Ariel watched their sister.

She's here but not here, thought Flame. What has happened to her? What did Zak do? She thought back to when she had run from the house to find Marina and Zak. They were down at the stables; Ariel and Ash had insisted they go with them to see the guinea pigs and rabbits. Nothing had seemed amiss and, for a while, Flame wondered if her anxiety about Zak was getting the better of her; that was, until she saw Marina sitting at the supper table. At first she thought her sister was tired from the afternoon's exertions, but when she noticed the glazed look in her eyes the alarm bell in her head started to ring.

Keen to get Marina alone, Flame, Ash and Ariel decided on an early night. Marina didn't seem bothered either way and was unaware that her sisters were all watching her as she climbed the stairs.

'You're all wonky,' said Ariel, following behind. Marina kept moving.

'Marina – you're all wonky,' repeated Ariel, louder.

Marina stopped and turned, slowly. 'Sorry, were you speaking to me?'

Ariel walked up beside her. 'Yes. I said, "You're all wonky".'

'What do mean "wonky"?'

'Well, you're not co-ordinated and you're leaning sideways.'

'Let's get Marina up to her room,' said Flame, taking her sister's arm.

As soon Marina got into her room, she flopped down on her bed. Flame turned on the bedside light, revealing an untidy room with piles of clothes and books all over the carpet. 'A Glorious Muddle', Marina liked to call it. Stepping over various things, Ash walked to the window and drew the curtains. Ariel sat down on the end of the bed.

Marina looked round at her sisters. 'Why have you all followed me in here? What's the matter?'

'Come and sit down, Ash,' said Flame. Marina drew up her legs as Ash sat down on the end of her bed beside Ariel. Flame sat down on the chair.

Marina gripped her forehead with both hands. 'Oh, my head – it feels all fuzzy,' she said.

Flame leaned forward and took her sister's hand. 'Marina, can you sit up and look at me,' she said, gently. Marina groaned and pulled herself up, awkwardly, into a sitting position. She sat back against the wall, her hands and arms floppy, her eyes glazed.

Flame came close to her sister's face. 'Marina, look into my eyes for a moment, will you.' Marina groaned again, but looked at Flame. Ash and Ariel leaned round.

'Oh my God,' said Ariel, her mouth dropping open. 'Marina's eyes are yellow!'

Flame stared at Marina's eyes: they were, indeed, yellow.

'That's exactly how Zak's eyes looked,' said Ariel.

'What do you mean my eyes are yellow?' asked

Marina, looking upset. 'What's happened? What sort of yellow?'

'It's not the whites of your eyes that have gone yellow, Marina, as they might if you had something wrong with your liver,' said Flame. 'It's the iris – where your eyes are usually blue, they've got a bright yellow cast.'

'But it's only at some angles,' observed Ash.

'And it's not all the time – I saw a flash, that's all,' said Flame.

Marina looked petrified. 'Have I got screeglings inside me or something?'

'No, no,' said Flame, in a soothing voice, although she did not know. Had Marina been bitten by a screegling? 'You know when you had that walk after the tennis match – did Zak touch you?' she asked.

'He didn't kiss me, if that's what you mean,' said Marina.

'Did he touch your hand?'

'Yeah, he held my hand for a bit. When Ash and Ariel ran up he let go. Why? What does that mean?'

Flame shook her head. 'I don't know, but something's happened. You didn't have yellow eyes or walk wonkily before he touched you.'

Marina gave a loud sob. 'I don't want yellow

eyes…' Holding her head in her hands, she began to cry.

Ash and Ariel sat against the wall beside her and put their arms around her. 'Don't worry, you'll soon feel better,' they said to her.

Flame grabbed some paper tissues and handed them to Marina. She looked on with an anxious face, trying to work out in her mind what had happened and why. Inside, she was seething. How dare this boy come into their house as a friend then hurt her sister. *How dare he!* As if the screegling invasion wasn't enough!

Marina cried for a few minutes and the sisters all felt very distressed. When she calmed down, Ariel looked at Flame and said, 'Does it mean that any girl Zak touches will go wonky?'

'I don't know, but it's probably because we have magic power.'

'You think Zak did this to me because I have magic power?' said Marina, wiping her eyes. 'Why would he want to hurt me? He *likes* me.'

Flame nodded, thoughtfully. 'I don't know, but there's definitely something odd about him.'

'What, like we're odd?' said Ariel. 'We look normal and we're not. Like that, you mean?'

'Yes,' said Flame, quietly. 'Like that.'

'Why did Zak hurt me?' asked Marina, and she

started to cry again. 'I don't want to have yellow eyes and feel wonky.'

'Maybe he didn't mean to,' said Ash. 'Perhaps he couldn't help it.'

'But he brought the screeglings here,' said Ariel, frowning.

'We don't know that,' said Ash. 'They may have been here already – and they drew Zak.'

'That's possible,' said Flame. That would mean there's another dark power at work, she thought to herself.

They were silent for a while. Then Ariel said, 'How do we know they're called screeglings?'

'That's what Sidney told you,' said Ash.

'Yes, but how does *he* know? Who told him about screeglings? Where do they come from? Have you ever seen anything in a book or on the telly about them?'

'If they're not known, then how would Sidney know?' said Ash.

Ariel looked at Flame. 'I've never heard of screeglings before, have you?'

Flame, who read widely, shook her head. 'No, I haven't.'

'So how does Sidney know?' said Ariel.

Flame shrugged. 'Perhaps you could ask him.'

'Yes, I will,' said Ariel.

They were silent again, then Ariel said, 'I wonder if anyone else round here has been invaded by screeglings?'

'I've a feeling they only go to places which have magic in them,' said Ash.

'So have they come here because it's Sprite Towers or because we're here?' said Ariel.

'It's probably both those things,' said Flame.

'Perhaps Zak's house was invaded,' said Ash.

'Maybe one of the screeglings bit him and he turned bad,' said Ariel. 'You know – then he went wonky, like Marina's gone wonky.'

At this, Marina gave another sob. 'I'm not wonky.'

'You'll soon feel better,' said Ash.

Flame looked at Ariel and smiled. 'You do say some funny things,' she said.

'But it could be true!' said Ariel.

Ash looked as if she was thinking deeply, then she said, 'So, do you think that people without magic power would see the screeglings?'

'That's a good point,' said Flame. 'Mum and Dad didn't see them. We didn't see them at first, in the daylight. What was it that Zak was trying to see?'

'Perhaps there are more screeglings up there,' said Ash. 'We didn't check the roof.'

'Yes, for the good reason that we can't get up there,' said Flame.

Marina leaned forward. Her eyes flashed a dull yellow and her sisters looked at her with alarm. 'They're still here,' she said, in a dull voice. 'I can feel them.'

'Can you see them in your mind?' asked Flame.

Marina nodded, her eyes now glazed.

'Where are the screeglings, Marina?'

She looked up at the ceiling. 'Up there,' she whispered.

'On the roof?'

Marina nodded.

'Are there lots of them?' whispered Ariel.

Marina shook her head slowly, from side to side.

Ash pulled her magic stone out of her pocket. It glowed a sickly yellow. 'And we thought we'd got rid of them …'

'How will we get onto the roof?' said Flame.

Ariel smiled. 'That's easy. I can fly up there.'

'You are absolutely NOT to go up to the roof on your own!' said Flame, sitting bolt upright and looking hard at Ariel. 'Do you understand?

Ariel blinked.

'Ariel, I'm serious,' said Flame, her face reddening. 'You must promise us you won't fly up to the roof unless we're with you. Do you promise?'

'I promise,' said Ariel, thinking how terrifying Flame could be when she got cross. But her eldest sister was right. Ariel sighed and leaned back against the wall.

'We can't go up there in the daylight – people might see us,' said Flame. 'And we can't go with Mum and Dad about. We'll have to go tomorrow night, when they've gone out, and hope that Grandma doesn't come back till Sunday. I think she'd be very upset to know we've been using our magic power again after we'd promised Mum not to.'

'We haven't had any choice,' said Ash. 'Surely she'd understand that.'

'Maybe,' said Flame. 'Anyway, I'd sooner she didn't know.' She looked at Marina, who still looked bleary. 'How are you feeling now?'

Marina nodded slowly. 'Yeah, I'm okay.'

'We must make the Circle of Power around her,' said Ash.

'We still don't know who sent the screeglings, if it wasn't Zak,' said Ariel.

'I know,' said Flame. 'There's a lot to find out here. But first, we must get Marina back to normal.'

Ash sat up. 'Do you remember what Mrs Duggery told us, when she first came here? You know, when Glenda Glass was breaking apart the roof, and we thought Sprite Towers might collapse. You remember that?' The others murmured, 'Yes.'

'She said, "You must stay close and work together". Remember? And she also said, "Find your balance and you'll find your power".'

Flame smiled. 'Yes, I remember. Mrs Duggery was right, as always, and we need to do that now.' She got up, clambered onto the bed and sat down facing Marina. Ash and Ariel turned sideways, so that the three girls formed a rough circle around Marina. Then they took hold of each other's hands and shut their eyes.

'We call in the Circle of Power,' said Flame, in a soft voice. 'We connect to come into balance. We come together to help our sister, Marina.'

For a few seconds nothing happened, then suddenly a band of blue light flashed around them in a circle. Ash and Ariel held on tight to Marina's hands. Flame opened her eyes and watched her sister, as the blue light grew more powerful and spread over their heads. Marina closed her eyes and her face began to relax. When she opened her eyes their colour was a bright, clear blue.

The sisters held the Circle of Power for another minute. They had just finished and let go of each other's hands when there was a sharp tap at the door and Ottalie put her head around. Quickly the Sprite Sisters moved apart.

'You look as if you're having a séance,' said Ottalie, walking into the bedroom.

'We were just making sure Marina was okay,' said Flame, climbing off the bed. Ash and Ariel got up too.

'I just came to see how you were, sweetie,' said Ottalie. She sat down on the bed beside Marina and stroked her thick, curly dark hair.

'I'm feeling much better, thank you, Mum,' said Marina.

'Yes, you look a lot better – that's good. So are you all off to bed now?'

'I'm going to go and read,' said Flame. 'Night Mum,' she said, as she leaned over to kiss her mother. 'Me, too,' said Ash and kissed her.

'I'll come and tuck you in,' Ottalie said to Ariel.

'Okay, Mum,' said Ariel.

'Night, Marina,' called her sisters as they left the bedroom.

A few minutes later, Marina was lying in bed ready to sleep. She lay in the darkness thinking. The wonky feeling had passed and her mind felt clear. She remembered how she had used her power of the South, the place of the heart and the emotions, to put back the feeling of heart into Sprite Towers after they had won the battle with Glenda Glass on that stormy July night, two years ago. When we've rid Sprite Towers of the

remaining screeglings I shall do that again, she thought
to herself. I shall put back the heart into this house and
we will forget about the invasion.

With that, Marina snuggled under her yellow duvet
and went to sleep.

Along the corridor Flame sat under her red duvet,
reading. She put the book down and stared across her
bedroom, thinking. How do we find out if Zak has magic
power without letting on to him that we have? We can
never tell him we have magic power: we have to keep
that a secret. No one outside the Sprite family must ever
know. But what sort of power is his? And who or what
sent the screeglings, if it wasn't Zak? Maybe Mrs
Duggery will send us a ghostly sign, she thought, as she
put down her book and turned off her bedside light.

Chapter Nineteen
Saturday
SOMETHNG IN
THE SHADOWS

'If there are screeglings on the roof we wouldn't smell them, would we? I mean, their pong would be blown away by the wind.' Ariel looked up at Sprite Towers. The roof was a long way up: around sixteen metres from the ground. She and Ash were standing on the lawn, far enough away to get a look at the big house. Nearby, Archie was chewing a stick and shaking it about, which was making a mess over the grass.

'Did you land on the roof, when you flew over the house?' asked Ash.

Ariel shook her head. 'No. It's massive – like a huge, rolling sea with the pantiles going up and down. There are valleys and flat bits running in between the different sections of the roof and there are massive chimneybreasts all over the place.'

'So, plenty of places for screeglings to hide,' said Ash, with a thoughtful look on her face.

'Yes, plenty of hiding places.'

Having finished their breakfast, Flame and Marina

came out of the kitchen door and walked towards them. Archie jumped up, his tail wagging.

'Can you see anything?' asked Flame, stroking Archie's shiny black head.

'Nope,' said Ariel.

'It's so high up there,' said Marina. She looked at Ariel. ' I can't believe you flew over Sprite Towers.'

Ariel smiled. 'I was just telling Ash that the roof is massive and rolls up and down, like the sea.'

'How are we all going to get up there?'

'Like we did when we had to get over the wall – I'll take you,' said Ariel.

'But whoever goes first is going to be up there alone, till the others come,' said Marina.

'I'll go first,' said Flame.

'No, I'll go first,' said Ash.

'But I'm older – I should go.'

'I can bind the screeglings, so they can't move.'

Flame bit her lip. 'Hm,' she agreed. 'Good point.'

'I'll take my magic stone, so I'll know if there's a screegling close by,' said Ash.

'Alright, but let's hope you don't see any till we're all up there together.'

'Thank heavens it's not raining,' said Marina.

'The tiles will still be slippery though, so we must take care climbing about,' said Flame. 'We'll need to be sure-footed – don't move quickly, whatever you do.'

'It's going to be a dark night with all this cloud,' said Ash.

'We'd better each take a torch,' said Marina.

'And dress up warm – it'll be cold up there tonight,' said Flame.

They were silent for a while, each looking up, their keen eyes focused on the gutters, the chimneys – anywhere they might be able to spot a screegling.

'We wouldn't see any screeglings from here, not in the daylight,' said Ash.

'I can't see anything,' said Marina.

'Nor me,' said Ash.

'What time do we go?' asked Ariel.

'As soon as Mum and Dad have left at half seven, surely,' said Marina.

'They may come back for something, so we can't go immediately,' said Ash.

'We can get dressed and ready though,' said Marina.

'It'll be dark by half past eight, especially on a cloudy night,' said Flame. 'I reckon we could leave at eight o'clock. Mum and Dad said they'd be back around midnight; we'd better be in bed by half eleven, in case they're home early.'

'So that gives us three and a half hours,' said Ash.

'Surely we won't need all that time,' said Marina.

Flame shrugged. 'But we may.'

'Do you think the screeglings that are up there will look like the ones we found in the house?' said Ariel.

'Why do you say that?' said Marina, turning to her sister.

Ariel shrugged. 'Well, if they've got dark magic – Sidney said they were half-goblin …'

Flame turned to look at Ariel, her face troubled.

Ariel carried on. 'They disappear in the daylight, don't they? They vanished in the Wild Wood. So why couldn't they change shape?'

Flame bit her lip. 'It's possible, pumpkin. Anything is possible. We have no real idea of what we're up against or why.'

Ariel crinkled her nose and turned to her big sister. 'You haven't called me "pumpkin" in yonks.'

'Haven't I?'

'You always used to call me that – and now you never do.'

'Well, I'm calling you it now, so what are you worried about?'

'Just stay being nice to me, please.'

'I'm always nice,' said Flame, with a look of mild outrage.

Marina and Ash burst out laughing. 'Now that *is* funny!' said Marina. Ariel giggled. Flame flicked back her long, copper hair. 'Huh,' she muttered.

It was twilight. The moon in its last quarter was hidden behind the thick band of low cloud that covered Sprite Towers. A cool wind blew, but the rain had gone and the grass was damp, not wet, underfoot as the Sprite Sisters walked over the lawn. Dressed in jackets, thick jumpers and hats, they each carried a torch. In Ash's jeans pocket was the magic stone; in Flame and Marina's pockets were their mobile phones. Ottalie and Colin had departed, Archie was locked in the house and they were ready to find out what was on the roof.

'It's so dark,' said Ariel, looking round.

'I'm not sure if that'll be a good thing or a bad thing,' said Ash. 'We'll have to listen hard and use our sense of smell to guide us.'

A brown owl screeched in the Wild Wood and the four Sprite Sisters started. Their four hearts began to pound as they looked up at the big house.

Goodness, the roof is such a height, thought Flame. What was up there? Would they all come down safely? What would happen if there was an accident? Would Ash be okay on her own until they joined her? She drew in a sharp breath and braced herself. Focus, she thought to herself. Focus.

Marina's heart was pounding. Apart from the height

of the roof, the thought of seeing another screegling frightened her. She looked round at Flame, saw her older sister was bracing herself, standing tall. Be strong, she told herself. Be strong.

Ash's face was tense, but she was determined to stay calm, to stay clear. 'We must be alert,' she said.

'And don't anyone go near the edge,' said Flame.

Ariel looked even smaller than usual with her beanie hat drawn over her head and her padded jacket. Her eyes were wide with excitement as she held out her hand to Ash. To her, this was a great adventure.

The four sisters stood on the lawn facing the west side of the house. Flame and Marina stepped back, as Ash took her sister's hand. Ariel closed her eyes and focused her mind. Then, opening her eyes, she summoned her magic power of Air. A second later, as if a wind had swept under them, the two girls lifted up. Higher and higher they rose into the darkening sky. On the lawn, Flame and Marina clutched each other as they watched as their sisters disappear over the top of the house.

'I hope they've landed safely,' said Flame.

'It's such a long way up there,' said Marina.

'And Heaven knows what's up there.'

'Ash will be alone. Where are they? They must have landed by now …'

'Relax, we must relax,' said Flame. 'Breathe out hard, Marina, then in slowly.' Marina did as she was told and a moment later loosened her grip on Flame's arm.

Then Ariel appeared, flying over the roof. She landed on the grass close by.

'Is Ash okay?' asked Flame.

Ariel nodded, breathless. 'It's slippery and very dark up there.'

'I'll go next,' said Flame. She turned to Marina and looked her in the eye. 'Stay strong.'

'I will,' said Marina, now completely focused on the task ahead.

As soon as Ariel caught her breath, she took hold of Flame's hand. Then they were rising, rising in the air. Flame felt the wind against her face and looked up as the big brick house loomed towards them. Higher and higher they rose, with nothing beneath them but air. Then they were above the roof and dropping down to a flat area, where the front part of the house butted onto the back section. Flame caught a glimpse of Ash's white face in the darkness, then Ariel was telling her to watch out. Suddenly, she felt her feet touch something solid and they were standing on the lead sheeting in the middle of the roof. For a few seconds Flame felt dizzy and disorientated.

Ash came up to her and took her arm. 'Are you okay?' she said.

Flame nodded and caught her breath. Gradually she felt her feet and got her bearings. 'It's so strange to feel weightless as you fly,' she said.

Ash laughed. 'Yes, it's weird – but wonderful, all the same.'

Flame looked around. Ariel had disappeared. 'Ariel's gone to get Marina,' said Ash. 'They won't be long.'

'Where on earth do we start?' said Flame, looking up at the massive expanse of pantiles rising up on both sides. 'I can't imagine how we're going to climb over that lot. And look at the size of these chimneys – you'd never guess how big they were from the ground. It's really creepy up here.'

Ash nodded. 'I keep expecting something to jump out at me.'

Flame shuddered.

Ash shone her torch along the valley. 'I think we'll have to stick to the flat bits – it's too dangerous to try to climb over the tiles.'

'Depends on where the screeglings are – unless they come to us.'

'We'd better let the magic stone guide us,' said Ash.

Flame shone her torch as Ash held out the magic

stone in the palm of her hand. A dull yellow light pulsed slowly through the stone.

'Looks like we're not alone,' said Flame.

'It's been doing that since I got up here,' said Ash.

'Are the screeglings close?' said Flame.

'I dunno yet, but they are here,' said Ash.

Suddenly there was a great whoosh of cold air as Ariel and Marina came flying down onto the roof. Flame and Ash jumped back as their sisters landed in a heap beside them.

'Are you okay?' asked Flame and Ash, pulling Marina and Ariel up into a sitting position. Marina looked giddy and startled.

Ariel looked dazed. 'Phew,' she said. 'That was really something to get you all up here.'

'I'll bet,' said Flame.

'It was an incredible feeling moving through the air,' said Marina.

'Let's sit down for a bit and get our bearings,' said Flame, bending her long legs beneath her and lowering herself onto the lead sheeting. 'Your eyes will soon get adjusted to the dark.'

Ariel sat down, pale-faced. She turned on her torch and shone the beam along the line of the north roof.

Gradually Marina came to. She reached into her jacket pocket and pulled out her torch and turned it on.

'So where do we start?' she said.

'Ash's magic stone is glowing yellow,' said Flame.

'So we know there is something up here,' said Marina.

'Yes.'

Marina bit her lip. 'I s'pose that just confirms what we suspected.'

Flame nodded. 'Yep.'

'I think we should follow the stone and see which way the light gets stronger,' said Ash.

Beside them something scuttled past. The Sprite Sisters nearly jumped out of their skins.

'What was that?' cried Ariel, swinging her torch round.

They leapt up and stood shining their torch beams this way and that. 'Can you see anything?' they asked each other. No, none of them could. Their hearts were pounding now.

'It didn't smell like a screegling,' said Ash. 'It was probably a rat.'

'What does your stone say now?' asked Marina.

In Ash's hand, the dull yellow light pulsated more strongly through the stone. 'They're getting closer,' she said. 'I think we should move that way.' She held her hand up towards the east side of the house.

'Okay,' said Flame. Holding her torch in front of

her, she stepped carefully across the lead sheeting that ran between the front and back halves of the roof.

'All okay at the back there?' she called.

'All okay,' her sisters answered.

'Keep your wits about you,' said Flame.

It took a minute to reach the east wall of the house. In front of them, along the edge, ran a brick parapet that stood half a metre high. Gingerly, the Sprite Sisters moved towards the parapet and looked out. Below them were trees and dark fields. In the distance, the lights of the village twinkled. The headlights of a car moved along the lane.

'It's weird to think that people are down there, doing normal Saturday night things like driving to the pub and watching telly,' said Marina.

'While we stand on a high roof in the dark, waiting to find screeglings,' said Ariel.

'Nobody would think to look for us here,' said Ash.

'Thank you, Ash, for that comforting thought,' said Marina.

Ariel turned back to look at the roof. Beside them, the East Tower loomed in the darkness. In every direction, huge expanses of pantiles rose and fell.

Ash turned back, too, and Flame and Marina followed.

'It's so dark up here,' said Marina.

'It's too early for the moon to be out,' said Flame. 'Even though my eyes have adjusted, I can't see anything unless it's in the direct beam of my torch.' She shone it at one of the chimneys. The intricate brick weave patterns that ran around it looked like a crazy face.

'Hey, the light in the stone is getting stronger,' said Ash. 'Whatever it is, is getting closer.'

With a rising sense of panic, the sisters swung their torches along the roof in every direction.

'How many screeglings do you think there'll be?' asked Marina.

'I don't know, but stay close together,' said Flame.

But Ariel, who either had not heard or chose not to, had moved along the parapet towards the East Tower. Less nervous of heights than her sisters, she did not mind the huge drop beside her.

'Ariel, come back!' shouted Flame.

As Ariel heard this, the rank odour of screegling wafted past her nose. She was just about to warn her sisters when something caught her eye on the ground just beneath her. What's that, she wondered, turning towards the parapet and squinting down into the darkness. It's a person walking over the grass. Someone is down there. Ariel stood transfixed.

She drew breath to alert her sisters and, at the same

time, heard the sound of clicking behind her. With a cry, she spun round. Edging towards her from behind the East Tower was a huge screegling. As it rose up on its back legs, the screegling stood as tall as she did. Ariel heard her sisters scream as two huge black claws reached down to clutch her in their grasp. Two round, dull yellow eyes stared at her, hypnotically, and the stench was overwhelming.

Ariel could not move. She could not breathe. With her feet close to the edge of the parapet, she stood transfixed, like a rabbit held in the headlights of a car. She could hear the screams of her sisters, but it felt as if they were far away. All she could see were the yellow eyes, the glistening slime dripping from the screegling's gaping jaws and the huge black claws.

Then, giving a piercing scream of terror, she felt herself falling – falling through the air.

Chapter Twenty

THE BATTLE ON
THE ROOFTOP

In a split second, the monster screegling lurched forwards. Shaking like leaves, Flame, Marina and Ash held out their right hands and summoned their magic power. Flame sent a bolt of Fire, Marina used her power of Water to turn the screegling to ice and Ash tried to bind it with her power of Earth.

The screegling stopped, its huge black claws suspended in the air. Gasping for breath, the Sprite Sisters stared at the monster – but a few seconds later, the screegling began to move again. With incredible speed, it lunged at the sisters. They jumped back, screaming in fright.

'We haven't stopped it!' shouted Marina.

'Careful – mind the edge!' cried Ash, as she hurled a bolt of her power of Earth at the screegling.

'Do it again, Ash!' yelled Flame, at the same time trying to send her power of Fire at the monster. Still the screegling moved forward.

'We can't stop it!' cried Marina.

'Yes, we can!' shouted Ash, moving slightly

forward. With all her might, she gathered her power to bind the monster. The screegling lurched forward, its huge claws ready to grasp her head. In the nick of time, Ash's power stopped it in its tracks. Flame hurled another bolt of her power of Fire and Marina sent shards of ice through the shiny black carapace.

'*Get back!*' screamed Marina, as the screegling swayed on its legs. The three sisters quickly moved back as the huge black body crashed down onto the roof.

A hissing, sizzling noise came from the screegling – and suddenly, all was still. Gasping for breath, their hearts pounding, Flame, Marina and Ash watched in horror. They waited. Would the screegling move again? The screegling remained immobile, its huge black legs crumpled, slime dribbling out of its jaws.

Terrified and shocked, the three sisters grabbed hold of each other and burst into tears. 'Where's Ariel?' 'What happened to her?' 'She may be dead!' they cried. Carefully, they moved to the edge of the parapet and shone their torches onto the ground.

Nothing. There was no sign of Ariel, but in the now inky black night they could see nothing in any direction. Exhausted and frightened, the three girls burst into tears and sank onto the roof. There they might have stayed, had the sound of clicking not warned them that the screegling was beginning to move again. As it dragged its legs underneath it, the huge creature started to pull itself upright.

Screaming with shock, the sisters jumped to their feet.

'But we killed it!' shouted Marina, her right hand extended and ready to deliver more magic power.

'I don't believe it!' shouted Ash, and she sent another bolt of her binding power. The screegling stopped moving and sank once more. The three sisters stood, rigid with terror, but the screegling did not move.

'We're trapped,' said Ash, her voice hoarse with tension.

'We've got to destroy it,' said Flame. 'We must.'

'How did it get so big?' whispered Marina, shining her torch on the screegling's dripping jaws.

'I don't know, but it must have very strong dark magic,' said Flame.

'We need Ariel,' said Ash. 'We need the four of us to defeat it.'

Though terrified by the huge drop, Marina inched towards the edge of the parapet and looked down. 'She could be dead, lying on the ground. I can't see anything … it's so dark …'

'Marina, we need to concentrate on the screegling,' said Flame. 'Otherwise we'll all be dead.'

'But we're stuck!' cried Marina, turning to her

sister. 'Even if we destroy it, we can't get down!'

'Let's worry about that when we've dealt with this.'

Another click from the screegling made Marina spin round so quickly, she almost fell over. As she regained her balance, the screegling was pushing itself up once more.

'Get back!' shouted Flame, grabbing Marina's shoulder.

The three sisters edged back as the screegling let out a blast of its terrible stench. For a moment, they could hardly breathe.

'Cover your mouth!' shouted Flame. Coughing and spluttering, they continued to inch backwards along the east parapet.

'Come back – get round here!' shouted Ash, reaching the corner and turning into the gulley that ran through the middle of the roof. This was where they had been standing when they first arrived and here, at least, they were not in danger of falling. On either side rose huge slopes of pantiles. All around them loomed the massive brick chimneys.

With their hearts pounding in their chests, their heads splitting with anxiety, they waited for the screegling to appear. In the darkness, all was still.

'Where is it?' said Flame, swinging the beam of her torch over the south roof.

'Perhaps we've killed it,' said Marina, shining her torch along the line of a chimney.

Ash pulled her magic stone out of her pocket. It pulsated quickly, emitting a sickly yellow light. 'The stone says it's still here,' she said.

'I can't believe we haven't killed it,' said Marina. 'All that magic power we hurled at it …'

'So where is it now?' said Flame, shining her torch down the valley. 'Is it following us?'

'Perhaps it's made itself smaller,' said Ash.

'There may be more than one of them,' said Flame.

'Oh no, I can't bear it,' cried Marina. 'What on earth shall we do?'

The three girls slumped down, tired, cold and very upset. Their little sister had fallen off the roof and they were trapped by a foe they could not defeat.

'Can you use the stone to direct us?' said Flame.

'Yes, but we'd be safer to wait here and let the screegling find us,' said Ash.

'Which it will,' said Marina.

'We're the bait,' said Ash.

Flame gave a grim laugh. 'Live Sprite – yum.'

'Can you use the stone to tell which side it will come from?' asked Marina.

'Let's stand in a circle, back to back, so we're all looking outwards,' said Flame. They moved together and stood in a tight circle. Ash held out her stone to the east side of the house.

'I don't think it's that way,' she said, softly.

'That's where it was when we left it a little while ago,' said Marina.

'Well, it ain't there now.'

They shuffled round ninety degrees, clockwise, until Ash was facing south. The huge expanse of pantiles rose in front of her. She held out her hand again. The stone gave out no light. 'Nope,' she said. They shuffled around another ninety degrees, so that Ash was facing west along the gulley. Again, nothing, but when they moved so that Ash was facing north, the stone began to pulse fast and emit a strong yellow light. 'I think it's up there,' she whispered.

Marina and Flame turned towards the north side of the roof. In front of them rose a massive slope of pantiles. At either end were the towers. To their left was the West Tower; to their right the East Tower. In between loomed the chimneybreasts.

'What do we do?' Flame wondered aloud. Moving the beam of her torch slowly, she scanned the chimneys on the north roof.

Marina took a deep breath. 'When we got rid of the screeglings in the house, Ash bound them, I put shards of ice through them and you sent your laser beam of Fire.'

'That's what we were trying to do here,' said Ash.

'But it's not working – this screegling is too powerful,' said Marina. 'We're missing something. We need to find another type of power. Can the stone tell us?'

Ash blinked. 'I don't know. I've never asked it stuff like that.'

'Well, try!'

'Say you would like two pulses for a "yes" and one for a "no",' said Flame. 'Come on, we need to hurry. The screegling could be back any second.'

'What am I asking?' said Ash.

'Ask it if we three sisters can destroy it,' said Marina.

Ash drew in a sharp breath. Staring at the magic stone, she said, 'Do we three Sprites have the power to destroy the monster screegling?'

Their hearts thudded in their chests. Pale-faced, they waited, but the stone gave no light, made no noise. Ash asked again, saying this time, 'At the moment, do we three Sprites have the power to destroy the screegling?'

The stone beeped once. 'No. The stone says no,' said Ash, her eyes wide.

'Not at the moment – that's the key,' said Flame.

'What is it we need?' said Marina, feeling her stomach rising up into her mouth.

Flame sighed long and hard. 'We need Ariel.'

'She may be dead,' whispered Marina.

'Ask that! Ask the stone if Ariel is alive,' said Flame.

Ash's hand shook. Her voice trembled. 'Is … is Ariel alive?' she whispered.

The three sisters stared at the stone.

'It's not telling me,' whispered Ash. Marina gave a sob and covered her mouth with her hand. Flame cried, 'No, no,' and turned away.

Ash still stared at the stone. 'Just wait,' she said.

Suddenly, as if from out of nowhere, they heard the sound of clicking.

Marina swung her torch. 'Mind out!' she cried.

The three sisters dived sideways as the monster screegling sped down the pantiles of the north roof. Flame jumped one way and fell onto her side, dropping her torch. Marina and Ash jumped the other and landed in a heap, their torches gone, too. In between them, the monster screegling stood up on its legs and breathed out its foul gas. Two massive claws lunged towards Marina and Ash. Screaming, they edged back in the dark.

Flame scrambled to her feet and waved her arms. 'Here!' she shouted, trying to divert the screegling's attention from her sisters. As the yellow eyes swung round to face her, Marina and Ash jumped up as fast they could. The screegling lunged towards Flame. At that moment, Ash held up her hand and sent a bolt of her power of Earth into the middle of the screegling's back. The power surged out of her fingers – and the screegling stopped still.

The girls gasped for breath, waiting for it to move again.

'Shrink it, Marina – for heaven's sakes shrink it!' said Flame, coughing.

Wobbly on her feet and spluttering, Marina held out her hand and sent a bolt of power into the monster screegling. The shiny black carapace started to shrink. Summoning her magic power of Water, Marina sucked out every bit of fluid in its body. The sisters watched in amazement as the screegling shrank smaller and smaller, until it became the same size as the ones they had seen in the house. The screegling made a long hissing sound and a thin trail of acrid yellow smoke rose in the air. Quickly, Ash bound it with her magic power, then Flame sent her laser-like power of Fire.

There was not a second to lose. 'Torches – find the torches,' said Flame. For the next minute, they scrabbled around on their hands and knees in the dark. As soon as Ash found one torch, they used the light to find the others. One by one the sisters found their torches. Of Ariel's torch, however, there was no sign.

'Maybe it fell with her,' said Marina.

The three girls huddled together.

'We can't rest for long,' said Flame. 'There may be other screeglings up here. What does the stone say, Ash?'

Ash held the round, brown stone in her outstretched palm. It continued to emit a steady pulse of sickly yellow light. The three sisters stared at it with a sense of hopelessness.

'I don't believe it,' said Flame.

'The magic stone says we can't destroy them. We can only immobilise them,' said Ash.

'How long have we got before the screegling grows bigger again?' said Marina.

'I've no idea, but we can't keep this up much longer,' said Flame. 'We're exhausted.'

'We need to find out what's happened to Ariel.'

'I know, but we can't leave this thing on the roof,' said Flame. 'It could come alive again and come into the house.'

'We can't get down anyway – at least not till the fire service puts up a very long ladder,' said Ash.

'So we're stranded with a monster screegling,' said Marina.

They fell silent. The darkness felt oppressive.

The roof looked bigger. The cold seemed to bite right through them.

'I'm cold,' said Ash.

'I'm worried about Ariel,' said Marina.

'We all are,' said Flame.

'What time is it?' asked Ash.

Marina pulled her mobile phone out of her pocket, 'Just gone ten o'clock.'

'We've been up here for ages,' said Ash.

'Mum and Dad will be home in an hour or so,' said Flame.

'We don't have to stay here: we can phone for help,' said Marina. 'I can do it now.'

'We *can't* phone for help – we'd have to explain what we were doing up here,' said Flame. 'And how are we going to explain how we got up here?'

'I'm not worried about that,' said Marina. 'Ariel may need help. She's more important than anything.'

'We must wait,' said Flame, her voice rising.

'Why?' asked Marina. 'What for? I could phone the fire service now.'

'No – please don't!' said Flame. 'I just have the feeling we should wait.'

'Is this one of your "feeling" feelings'?

Flame nodded, wearily. 'Yep.'

'Well, I don't want to spend a second more than I've

got to up here, with that vile creature chasing us and our sister lying hurt below,' shouted Marina.

'Nor do I – but we can't leave it. Not now. We have to finish what we've come to do,' said Flame.

'For heaven's sake, Flame, the magic stone has told us we're not strong enough to finish off the screegling! Let's just go down and see what's happened to Ariel. We can always come back another time.'

'If you ring the fire service and they bring us down from this roof, Mum will never let us out of her sight again,' said Flame, through gritted teeth. 'Is that what you want?'

Marina looked really angry. 'So what do you suggest then?'

The two sisters looked at one another.

'Whatever,' said Marina, turning away. 'First of all I'm going to call down to Ariel.'

'Don't go near the edge,' said Flame, but Marina was already moving along the gulley towards the east wall.

Ash stepped forward. 'Hang on, Marina – I've an idea.'

'What?' said Marina, turning round.

'We could make a Circle of Power, up here, and call Ariel in our heads,' said Ash. 'If she hears us in her head, she'll answer – and we'll know where she is and what's happened.'

'And if she can't answer?' asked Marina.

'Ariel will hear us – and she will tell us. Let's just try.'

Marina shrugged. 'Okay,' she said. 'But I can't see how we can make a Circle of Power without Ariel.'

'We've got to watch out for the screegling,' said Flame. 'It could come hurtling back at any minute.'

'Okay, so we don't close our eyes,' said Ash. 'But let's just see if this works.'

The three girls shuffled together in the darkness and stood, back-to-back and holding hands.

'If this doesn't work, I don't know what on earth we'll do,' sighed Flame.

'Come on, let's clear our minds and think about the Circle of Power,' said Ash. 'Think about Ariel and all call her in your head.'

'Tell her we need her,' said Flame.

Marina took a deep breath, drew back her head and shouted as loudly as she could into the darkness, 'A-R-I-E-L!'

Flame and Ash jumped with surprise.

'I didn't mean to shout out!' said Ash.

'No, but I did,' said Marina. And she shouted again, 'A-R-I-E-L …'

Chapter Twenty-One
A HAND IN THE DARKNESS

Ariel opened her eyes. She was looking up at the pitch-dark sky and seemed to be lying on something cold and damp. She reached out her hand and felt around her. Grass. She was lying on the grass. What had happened?

Someone was calling her. She could hear her name shouted through the darkness. There it was again: A-R-I-E-L ….

She pulled herself up into a sitting position, then rubbed her eyes with the back of her hands. Wake up. I must wake up, she thought. I must remember what happened – but she could not. Her memory was a blank, except for the sense of falling. For a few seconds, she had in her mind the sensation of cold air passing over her face and her arms out wide. Screaming – I remember screaming. But why was I falling? And what was I falling from?

There was the voice again. A-R-I-E-L. Ariel stood up. Her limbs felt heavy and ached as if they were bruised. In front of her the house towered in the darkness. The voice seemed to come from high up. Blearily, she looked up. Perhaps she fell from the roof – but why would she have been up there? Why was she standing in the dark wearing outside clothes and boots?

Ariel took in a few long, deep breaths of cold air. As she began to feel more awake, the faces of her sisters came into her mind. They're looking for me, she thought. Now she heard the voices again, but this time they were in her head. 'Ariel, we need you,' her sisters were saying and, 'Ariel, we're in danger. Come quickly – we must make the Circle of Power.'

Ariel tilted her head back and looked up. We were on the roof, she thought. That's where my sisters are. I must get up there.

Her mind went fuzzy again. I can't, she thought. It's too high and I haven't got a ladder. Oh dear, why is everything so blurry?

She shut her eyes and let her thoughts wander. The image of sitting in the blue cedar tree floated through her mind. Then she remembered standing on the grass and holding out her hands. That was it, she thought. I learned to fly!

Ariel opened her eyes. She felt clearer now, but still the ground felt wobbly underfoot. For a second she had the sense that she was not alone on the lawn – that there was someone nearby – but when she turned and looked about her she could see no one there.

I have to get to the roof. My sisters are in danger. There it is again. Why do I have the feeling that I'm not alone? Is someone watching me in the darkness? Focus, I must focus. What do I need to do? I need to fly to the roof …

She took in another deep breath and tried to steady herself. Little by little, the ground felt more solid until she felt it firm underfoot; then, with all her might, she focused her mind on her magic power. Better now. She could feel it; she was going to fly. Throwing her head back, she held out her hands wide and visualised herself flying through the air, up to the roof. With a sudden whoosh, she lifted up, felt her feet leave the ground and the cold air hit her face. Then she was moving, moving up through the darkness until she was flying high above the house.

Torches, she could see beams of light moving in the darkness. There they were, down there – her sisters, standing on the roof. Danger – there was danger, she remembered. For a brief moment, the image of huge black claws came to her and as her mind wandered she felt herself wobble in the air. Concentrate, she thought, suddenly unsteady.

Then she was back on a straight course, flying through the sky. At the same time, the sky cleared and the moon rose over Sprite Towers. Below, her sisters stood huddled in the darkness. With a great sweep, Ariel landed on the roof. As her feet hit the lead sheeting, a scream went up.

'Ariel!' her sisters cried, as they hugged her tight. 'Thank goodness, you're okay!' For the next minute the Sprite Sisters stood close, crying with relief.

'Thank heavens!' said Marina.

'You fell,' said Ash.

'I fell?'

'You fell off the roof,' said Flame.

'You were by the edge,' said Marina. 'You were looking over the parapet and suddenly you fell.'

'The screegling was about to get you,' said Ash.

'Screegling?'

'Don't you remember?' said Flame.

Ariel stared ahead. Did she remember? She shook her head.

'Did you fly?' said Ash. 'Is that how you saved yourself from the fall?'

Ariel shook her head. 'No – something caught me.'

'What do you mean something caught you?' said Marina.

Ariel looked blank. 'I don't know. I just know I was falling, then something caught me, then it all went blank.'

Ash, Flame and Marina looked at one another in the torchlight, their faces confused. 'But what?' they all asked.

Ariel shrugged and gave a big sigh. 'I just remember the feeling of whooshing through the air stopped and I knew I was safe. I woke up lying on the grass.'

Close by, a pantile knocked against another: it made a dull clunking sound. Instantly alert, Flame, Marina and Ash held up their torches.

'What was that?' they cried, peering into the darkness. Behind them, a shadow seemed to pass and they spun round again, now waving their torches in the opposite direction. It felt, suddenly, as if there were was something else around them. As the moon rose, it cast an eerie, silver light over the roof. Everywhere there seemed to be shadows. The Sprite Sisters waited, watching, breathing hard. On the roof beside them lay the shrivelled screegling.

'We must act quickly,' said Flame, her chest tightening with panic.

'Ariel, come on – we must make the Circle of Power,' said Marina, grabbing her little sister's sleeve. 'We have to get rid of the screeglings. Do you remember?'

Ariel nodded. The image of the claws flashed through her mind again. Suddenly she remembered the foul smell, the yellow eyes, the nasty black beetle things that had crawled through Sprite Towers.

'Yes, yes, I remember.'

'Come on then,' said Marina, and within a few seconds the sisters were standing in a small circle, facing each other and holding hands.

'The Circle of Power,' said Flame. A moment later, there was the blue light that Ariel knew so well: the blue light that would protect them and clear away anything that came to do them harm. The light grew stronger and stronger until it covered the four sisters in a huge ball of electric blue.

Ariel sank into the light, but one part of her mind wandered and her acute hearing alerted her to something moving nearby. Was that a footstep she could hear? She opened her eyes and turned her head. She had the sense that something or someone was watching them. She peered into the darkness.

There's something there, she thought. I can feel it. Is it another screegling?

At first, she could see nothing. Then, in the shadows, she distinguished the faint outline of a person.

Ariel gasped. It's a tall boy with spiky hair, she thought. Why is Zak standing there? Why is that ball of black light moving towards him? It's as if he's pulling it into his body …

Ariel dropped her sisters' hands and turned. 'Zak,' she called out. *'Zak?'*

'What? What's happening?' said her sisters, dropping their hands and turning round.

At that moment, the clouds parted. Moonlight shone down on Sprite Towers. The slopes and the valleys of the roof, the massive chimneys and the curving lines of the pantiles, were suddenly illuminated in bright, silvery light.

Standing across the roof was the boy with hawk-like eyes. As they saw him, the Sprite Sisters cried out in amazement – but in a flash he was gone.

'*Where is he?*' they cried, staring at the now empty roof.

'Did you see? Did you see the ball of black light?' shouted Ariel.

'*What?*' said her sisters.

'The *screegling* – Zak drew it towards him,' said Ariel. 'He pulled it into his stomach. It was like a ball of black light.'

'What?' said Marina, staring at her sister.

'But how?' said Ash.

Flame shone her torch over the roof to where Zak had been standing. Then she swung it back to the place where the shrivelled screegling had lain. 'The screegling has disappeared,' she said.

Ash held up the magic stone. It glowed a beautiful

bright blue. 'That's better,' she said, with a great sigh of relief.

'Has the screegling definitely gone?' said Marina.

'Yes,' said Ash.

'Then we're safe at last,' said Flame.

Ariel turned to look behind her at the great span of pantiles that formed the north slope of the roof. Her gaze moved from one chimney to another, but she could see nothing. 'He's gone,' she said. With a great yawn, she rubbed her eyes and said, 'It's all fuzzy.'

Marina put her arm around Ariel's shoulders. 'You need to rest,' she said. 'We need to get down.'

'We all need to rest,' said Flame. 'I'm exhausted.'

'I'm freezing,' said Ash.

'We must be in bed before Mum and Dad come home,' said Flame.

'What time is it?' asked Marina.

With the light from her torch, Flame looked at her watch. 'It's just gone eleven. Blimey, we'd better get going – Mum and Dad said they'd be back by midnight.'

'Don't panic,' said Marina. 'We've got time.'

Flame looked at Ariel. She seemed to be in a daze again. Flame frowned, worried. 'Ariel, are you feeling strong enough to take us down?'

As Ariel turned to Flame, her eyes focused.

'Yes, I'm ready – I'll fly you all down,' she said.

Ash went first and thrilled at the feeling of speeding downwards through the air. They landed with a thump on the lawn, then Ariel was off again, up into the night air. A minute later, Marina landed on the lawn. The two sisters waited, anxiously, until Flame and Ariel appeared above the parapet. A few seconds later, they landed on the grass.

'We're all safe,' said Flame. 'What a relief.'

As soon as they were in the house, Marina took Ariel up to bed. Flame got four glasses of water and made a hot water bottle for Ariel. Ash let Archie out for a run on the grass, then they were ready for bed. Carrying the glasses of water, Flame and Ash turned out the lights and climbed the wide mahogany staircase.

The older girls tucked Ariel into bed with her hot water bottle, then hastened to their rooms. Ten minutes after they had turned out their lights, Ottalie and Colin motored up the driveway.

Ariel lay in bed, her eyes wide open in the darkness. Hugging the hot water bottle, she tried to remember what had happened. It was all so fuzzy, but she felt certain that she had been caught as she fell off the roof. She remembered screaming as she fell. She remembered the terrifying feeling of hurtling towards the ground. Yet she had not hit the ground hard; she had landed gently.

Someone – she felt sure – had saved her from falling and laid her on the grass.

It was Zak, she thought. Zak caught me as I fell ...

With a big yawn, she closed her eyes and fell into a deep sleep.

Chapter Twenty-Two
Sunday
TEARS

Marina woke late and lay back against her pillows. The Sprites were a family who got up and got on in the morning. All except Marina, who liked her sleep, liked to lie in bed and would often read for hours. This morning she could hear from the voices and the doors opening and shutting that the family was busy below. Sunday morning was her mother's bread-making time. Ash would be in the garden with her father, lifting and picking vegetables. Flame would be helping to prepare the lunch and Ariel would be cleaning out the guinea pigs. Today the Sprites would have a special lunch, as Grandma would be home, having been away for several weeks.

For the moment, all that could wait. Marina wanted to think about the events of last night. She stared at the ceiling, her hands tucked behind her head and her face furrowed in concentration. Images and memories drifted through her mind. She and her sisters had shared some incredible experiences, but until now none of them had involved dark magic that came from outside the Sprite family. The screeglings were their first experience of this and it had been deeply unsettling. But the knowledge that Zak used dark magic troubled Marina more. Whilst she was drawn to the boy, intuition told her all along that she must judge with care.

Marina sighed. She knew – had known all along in some deep part of her – that this quiet, cool boy with his hawk-like eyes had some kind of magic power. She could feel it in him. She had hoped it would be a 'good' magic power, but there was nothing beneficial about the invasion of the screeglings. On the other hand, he had saved her sister from falling and he had taken away the monster screegling.

She propped herself up on her elbows and stared across the room. There were so many questions. If Zak brought the screeglings to Sprite Towers, why did he help to take them away? A small voice in her cried out that it was for her. She blew out hard and thumped back down on her bed. Nonsense, this was all nonsense. Zak was not involved. He had not called up the screeglings – they had come on their own …

Marina bit her lip. I want this to all go away, she thought. I want Zak to be a friend I can trust. I want this whole thing to be nonsense. But it was not nonsense. A lot of strange things had happened to her and her sisters in the last two years. It would be easy to dismiss these experiences, but despite being 'out of this world' on occasion, they had still happened. If Marina had learned anything, it was never to dismiss something because it did not fit accepted thinking. She had learned to always remain open. She had also learned that you don't deal with things by ignoring them.

Things felt complicated. If she did not care for Zak it would be different. Her attraction to him blinded her, in part – and it hurt. From the very first day he had visited Sprite Towers, Zak had used dark magic against them. How can I forgive him? Why would he hurt us? But if it was he who rescued Ariel – and *something* happened to help her, otherwise she would have been killed, as she would not have had time to use her magic power – then is he all 'bad'? If Zak wanted to *really* hurt us he would have left Ariel to fall to her death, then left me, Flame and Ash to slug it out with the monster screegling on the roof – a battle we could not win. But he didn't. He came to our rescue. And that means Zak has a heart …

At the thought of this, Marina smiled a smile that was at once happy and sad. Then she jumped out of bed, had a quick shower, dressed and ran downstairs. A hive of activity met her as she walked into the kitchen. Ash and Colin had come in from the garden with a pile of fresh vegetables, which they were placing on one end of the kitchen table. At the other end, Mum was kneading bread dough. Ariel was cleaning out the animal feed bowls in the utility room. Flame was putting the finishing touches to a huge meringue covered with cream and raspberries.

'Yum,' said Marina, eyeing the meringue and making a grab for a strawberry.

'Get off!' said Flame, batting her sister's hand away.

Mum looked up. 'Morning, darling,' she said, pushing her blonde hair back from her face with the back of her hand. 'Up bright and early again!'

Marina gave her mother a kiss on the side of her face. 'I need my beauty sleep,' she said.

'Huh,' said Flame. 'In that case, you should be miles more beautiful than any of us.'

Marina laughed. 'I am!'

Flame smiled. 'Says who?'

'Says me.'

'You would say that, wouldn't you!'

'Have you been an old slug-abed again, Marina?' said her father.

'I think sleep is greatly unvalued,' said Marina.

'What about lolling?' asked Flame.

'I wasn't lolling; I was deep in thought,' said Marina. The two sisters exchanged looks and both knew exactly what she had been thinking about. She was not the only one. Flame had been thinking about the matter of Zak as she worked in the kitchen. Ash had been thinking about it as she busied herself in the garden. Ariel was, as usual, in a dream, but still had part of her mind on the events on the roof.

A few minutes later, as Ariel carried the clean bowls back to the animal hutches, Marina ran after her over the lawn. 'Wait!' she called.

Ariel stopped and turned around. 'Hi,' she said.

'Hi,' said Marina. 'How are you feeling?'

'I'm fine, thanks.'

'You're not feeling wobbly?'

Ariel smiled. 'I'm okay, really.'

'That's a relief.'

'How are you feeling?' said Ariel, as they started to walk towards the stables.

Marina sighed. 'I've been thinking about what happened last night. Lying in bed gave me the chance to work things through in my mind.'

Ariel looked up at her sister. 'And?'

'And – I don't understand.'

The two sisters stopped walking and turned to face each other.

'What was it all about? Why would Zak want to hurt us?'

'I don't understand either,' said Ariel.

Marina sighed – a big sigh of disappointment.

'Flame and Ash think we need to decide what to do,' said Ariel.

'You've all been talking about it?'

'Yes, and we think we should summon Zak.'

Marina's face clouded. 'Yes, I agree.'

They walked in silence till they reached the hutches.

Marina watched Ariel open the doors and fill up the bowls with fresh food. 'I don't like confrontation,' she said, reaching in and picking up a guinea pig. With a sad face, she pulled the little animal towards her and stroked its head.

'No, but we must talk to Zak and find out what all this is about,' said Ariel, gently, aware that her sister suddenly looked absolutely wretched. As Marina burst into tears, Ariel took the guinea pig from her and put it back in the hutch.

'How *could* he?' sobbed Marina. 'That's what I can't understand. He came here as a friend – and what he's done is monstrous!'

'Come and sit down,' said Ariel, taking Marina's arm. They sat down together on a low brick wall and Ariel put her arm around her sister's shoulders.

Marina cried and cried, wiping her face with her hands, and snuffling into the tissues that she pulled out of her jeans pocket. Eventually she stopped crying and said, 'You realise that this means that there's magic out there in the world that we'll have to deal with?'

Ariel sighed. 'Yes, I've thought about that. Zak will be at school and he may use magic again.'

'I wonder what he wants from us?' said Marina.

'He can't be all bad or he wouldn't have stopped me from falling or helped us on the roof.'

'Maybe not, but he's bad enough to be connected to the screeglings and we can't trust him.'

'That's true.'

They sat silently for a while. Suddenly Marina burst out, 'I feel so *angry* with Zak!'

Ariel smiled. 'That's better.'

Marina smiled, then fell silent.

Eventually Ariel said, 'The good thing is we've all found our magic power again, don't you think?'

Marina nodded, half-heartedly.

'Flame is being much nicer to me, too.'

'You and Flame, honestly.'

'Well, you're almost as bad sometimes. I expect you'll be glued to your mobile as soon as this is all over.' She looked at Marina with worried eyes, then said, 'You will still talk to me, won't you?'

Marina laughed. 'Yes, of course, numpty.'

They were quiet again, then Marina gave a big sigh.

'I s'pose we'd better go back to the house. It's not long till lunch.'

They got up and began to walk over the lawn.

'You know, I think Zak must have recognised that we had magic power from the moment he met us,' said Marina.

'It makes me wonder how many people there are around who have magic powers without us knowing,' said Ariel.

Marina nodded. 'A lot more than we realise – and some have got good power and others have bad power.'

'It's scary.'

'Well, we'll face it together.'

'I'm really sorry that you've been so upset by Zak.'

'I know – thank you.'

'Perhaps he likes to play games.'

'Yes, I think he does.'

They stopped halfway across the lawn and looked up at the roof of the house.

Marina laughed. 'I can't believe we flew up there last night and fought a giant screegling! Nobody would ever believe us.'

Ariel smiled. 'Best we don't mention it then. Come on, let's go and have some lunch.'

As they got back to the house, Grandma and her

dachshund, Bert, arrived. There was much hugging and kissing as the family greeted Marilyn. Colin and Flame lifted her cases from the car and carried them into the house. Ash picked up Bert, kissed him on the head and stroked his long silky ears. Archie lolloped around Grandma, who bent down to stroke his head. Ash put Bert down on the ground and Archie immediately covered the little dog in big, slobbery licks.

'Archie's pleased that he's got his friend back,' said Ariel, and they all laughed.

'It's lovely to have you back, Grandma,' said her granddaughters.

'It's lovely to be back at last,' she said, giving each of them a hug.

'Welcome home, Mother,' said Colin, as they walked into the house.

Following behind, Flame whispered to her sisters, 'Not a word to Grandma about any of what's happened.' But as she said this, Flame felt something tighten in her chest. If they said nothing about the events of last week – Ariel's flying, the screeglings, Zak – it would be the first time since they had gained their magic power that the sisters had not told their grandmother about using it. For Flame this was particularly difficult, as the two had always been close, but Marina, Ash and Ariel were happy to defer to Flame's judgment on this matter. When they questioned her about it later, as Flame knew they would, she would say that it was one of her 'feelings' that they should keep quiet about their magic power from now on. 'We are old enough to deal with this ourselves,' she would say. Knowing that, her tension abated.

The Sprite family sat down to lunch feeling happy to be together. Every one of them appreciated the closeness of their family and the delicious food on their table. The four sisters looked around them with new eyes, aware that their lives had changed. Of all of them, Flame felt this most keenly. With her gift of far-sightedness, she could see that Zak's dark magic was the first of their tests. Soon they would be back at Drysdale's. No doubt, Zak would bring more dark magic. The sisters must stick together. They must always remember never to use their magic power to do harm to another human being.

As the conversation rattled on, Flame looked across the table and caught her grandmother's gaze. Their clear, green eyes met and Flame felt a new sense of assurance. For the first time in a long while, she felt she knew who she was and where she was going.

And the next thing she must do, as soon as lunch was over, was to summon Zak to meet with them. It was time to talk to the boy with hawk-like eyes.

Chapter Twenty-Three
Tuesday
THE RECKONING

The sky was inky dark and it was nearly midnight on Tuesday when Zak walked out of the Wild Wood. The Sprite Sisters were waiting at the camp.

'He's here,' whispered Ariel. The sisters got up from their chairs and peered into the shadows.

Zak walked towards the campfire. As he approached, his face gained definition and he looked at each of the sisters in turn. 'Flame, Ariel, Ash, good evening,' he said. Flame and Ash nodded in acknowledgement, their faces drawn. Ariel said, 'Hello.'

Then he looked at Marina and gave her a small smile. 'Marina,' he said. Her heart leapt as she caught his glance, but he turned away.

'Let's sit down,' said Flame, beckoning Zak to the empty chair beside her.

They all sat down around the fire. An hour before, the sisters had built it up with three big oak logs. Now the logs were burning red, the flames licked and spat and the smell of wood smoke filled the air. In the glow of the firelight, Zak's sharp features softened. He stared at the fire, silently.

The Sprite Sisters watched him, but he seemed in no hurry to speak.

It's as if his heart is heavy, thought Flame. She glanced at her sisters. Ash's face registered patience: she would wait until all was revealed. Ariel's expression was one of wide-eyed curiosity. Marina's eyes spoke of hope tinged with sadness.

What am I expecting, wondered Flame. What I expect and what I hope for are different. I hope for resolution; I expect complication.

She gave a big sigh and sat up in her chair. Sitting tall now, her green eyes focused and sharp, she turned to Zak and said, 'So.'

Zak turned to her, his eyes instantly alert. 'So,' he replied.

Ariel, Ash and Marina looked from Flame to Zak and Zak to Flame. The boy with hawk-like eyes and their tall, copper-haired sister were looking hard at one another. The three girls sat forward and held their breath.

Flame's eyes narrowed. 'You have brought pain and distress to my family and to me. Why?'

The side of Zak's lip curled. 'It's a game. It's just a game.'

Flame's expression turned to amazement, then fury. For an instant she looked as if she might jump up and sock Zak. *'A game?'* She spat out the words. 'You call that a *game*? Our parents poisoned, the house full of disgusting creatures, fighting on the roof with a giant screegling, Ariel's fall. *All that is just a game?'*

'Yes,' replied Zak, his voice level, his eyes focused on Flame.

Flame rolled her eyes upwards in disbelief, then she brought her gaze down to Zak and looked at him with a face like thunder. *'How dare you!* How dare you come to our house and pretend to be our friend – and all the time try to hurt us. *How dare you!'*

'Traitor,' said Marina.

'You betrayed our trust,' said Ash.

'I could have been killed,' said Ariel.

Zak nodded. 'Yes,' he said and stared at the fire.

The sisters looked from one to the other.

'But why?' said Ariel. 'What have we done to you, Zak?'

He turned to her. 'Nothing.'

'And?'

'And what?'

'I don't understand what you mean,' said Ariel. 'We've done nothing to hurt you. You came here as a friend. Why would you want to hurt us?'

Zak looked at Ariel long and hard. Then he said, 'You have done nothing to hurt me. But it's not about *doing* anything. It's about *being*.'

Marina, Ash and Ariel looked mystified.

Flame frowned. 'You mean, it's not what we do to you, but who we are.'

Zak nodded. 'Exactly.'

'You have magic power. When you come up against other magic power, you react. Is that what you are telling us?'

'Yes.'

Flame gave a derisory laugh. 'But that's like saying you can throw your toys out of the pram when you feel like it! The fact that you have magic power doesn't mean you should not control it and use it wisely. We all have to learn to take responsibility for our actions.'

'You're missing the point,' said Zak.

'The point being?'

Zak hesitated.

'You just said it was a game,' said Marina. Zak caught her glance and held it – but Marina looked away.

'Don't tell us you don't have a choice in how you use your power, Zak, because we won't believe you,' said Flame. Her voice was cold now and she gripped the sides of her chair.

Ariel crossed her arms and shot Zak an angry look.

'No, we won't,' she said.

A big spark burst out of the fire and landed near Zak's feet. The smouldering wood glowed red on the grass. Zak kicked it back towards the fire.

'You sit there mumbling – and that's it?' said Flame. 'It's not good enough, Zak. We want more – we demand some explanation for the hurt you have caused us. We would appreciate an apology.'

'I didn't have to come here tonight,' said Zak, leaning back in his chair.

Flame gave a cold laugh. 'But curiosity got the better of you, didn't it.'

Zak stretched out his legs and put his hands behind his head.

Flame bristled. 'You really think you are something.'

He looked round at her and said in a soft voice, 'I *am* something.'

'Who *are* you?' said Marina.

'Why have you moved here?' said Ariel.

'What do you really want from us?' said Ash.

'What is your power?' said Flame.

Zak held up his hands. 'One at a time,' he said. He looked at Marina. 'My name is Zak Ashthorpe. I am fifteen years old and I am the adopted child of Marie and John Ashthorpe.'

'You're adopted?' said Marina. 'You didn't say …'

'Do you love your adoptive parents?' asked Ash.

'Yes, very much.'

'Have you been happy at home?'

'Yes.'

'Have you got any brothers or sisters?' asked Ariel.

'No, just me.'

'Have your adoptive parents got magic powers?'

Zak laughed softly. 'No, they're not into anything "weird".'

Ariel looked at Zak and said, 'But it means you don't know who you really are.'

Zak shrugged.

'If you don't know who your natural parents are, you wouldn't know if they have – or had – magic powers,' said Flame. 'You wouldn't know where your power comes from.'

'No,' said Zak.

'Have you had anyone to talk to about your magic?' asked Flame.

Zak shook his head. 'Nope,' he said.

They were all silent for a moment.

'When did you find you had magic power?' said Marina.

Zak bit the side of his lip as he thought. 'When I was about ten, I guess. Somewhere round there.'

'How did you know?'

'Stuff started to happen around me.'

'Such as?'

'Things lifted up, broke and moved around me,' said Zak. 'I could hear what people were thinking.'

'Were you thrown out of school?' asked Flame.

'Why do ask that?' said Zak, with a direct look

Flame hesitated, then said, 'Because I see fire around you in my mind.'

Zak gave a short laugh. 'I was asked to leave – there was an accident in the chemistry lab.'

'A fire?'

Zak nodded. 'Yep.'

'You were expelled!' said Ariel, her mouth dropping open. The sisters looked from one to the other in alarm.

'Is that why you've come to Drysdale's?' said Ariel.

'You started a fire …' said Marina, shaking her head.

'Deliberately?' asked Ariel, her mouth tightening.

'No more than I brought the screeglings here,' said Zak, sitting forward. He gripped his nose between his fingers and rubbed it. Then he shrugged. 'It's more that stuff happens around me.'

'So is it a game – or is it not?' said Flame. 'You either control your power or you don't.'

'Which do you want us to believe?' said Ash, looking at Zak with her kind eyes.

Zak seemed to be touched by Ash's gentle tone. His face softened as he held her gaze, then he turned away with a look of confusion. 'I don't know,' he said.

They were silent again, until Flame gave an impatient sigh. 'Tell us about the screeglings.'

'How did you know about the screeglings?' said Ariel.

Marina shuddered. 'They were minging.'

'Are you drawn to dark power, Zak?' asked Flame. He nodded.

'I knew it,' said Flame.

'How did you know about the screeglings?' asked Ariel again.

'I like looking round second-hand bookshops,' said Zak. 'I found this really old book on magic. There was a tiny little bit about something called a screegling in there. It intrigued me. Then when we moved here, I found myself thinking about them. I started cycling round – had this feeling I could find these things called screeglings.'

'And you came here?' said Ash.

'Yes.'

'But if you knew they were dark magic, why would you look for them?' said Flame.

Zak gave her a withering look. 'Because I'm drawn to dark power, like I said.'

'And once you released the screeglings, you found you couldn't control them – is that it?'

Zak turned to stare at the fire.

Flame drew a sharp breath. 'It's one thing to be interested in something and another to inflict it on other people,' she said, her voice rising. 'You make me sick! Poor Zak can't help the fact that he has dark power and likes to hurt people. I'm not buying that – it's pathetic!'

'Sssh,' said Marina and Ariel together.

'Keep your voice down, Flame, or we'll have Dad down here wondering what's going on,' said Ash.

'And what about you, Miss Goody Two-Shoes,' said Zak. 'What about your magic power? Care to tell me about how you got rid of the screeglings?'

Flame was absolutely still. Marina, Ash and Ariel looked quickly from one to the other.

Marina turned to Zak, her face anxious. 'We can't talk about that, Zak.'

Zak snorted. 'Right.' He looked across at Flame and leaned forward, his elbows on his knees. 'I've seen your magic power, Flame. I've seen all of you use your power. I know what you sisters can do.'

The Sprite Sisters were silent. Forbidden to speak

of their magic power to anyone outside their family, they did not move.

Ariel turned to Zak and fixed her big grey eyes on his dark eyes. 'You're unkind, Zak,' she said. 'You've hurt us. You've hurt our parents. You're trying to make it out that you can't help what you do, but I agree with Flame. We can all help what we do.'

'You don't have to use dark power, Zak,' said Ash.

'I'm a boy – I'm curious. I like to test my power.'

Flame shook her head. Ash looked sad.

'There must be some good in you,' said Marina. 'You caught Ariel as she was falling. There must be good in you …'

Zak stared into the fire, watched the flames lick around the burning wood.

'We can't control the way things react to us, but we can choose the way we react to them,' said Marina.

'If you have good parents, you will know these things,' said Flame.

'I have good parents,' said Zak.

'Then listen to them!'

'Like you listen to yours about magic?' said Zak.

Flame started. 'We would never set out to hurt anybody, Zak – you know that.'

'Are you going to try to hurt us again?' said Ariel.

'I hope not,' said Zak.

'That's a stupid thing to say,' said Ariel.

Zak stared at the fire.

Flame stood up and walked around on the grass, this way and that, angry and tense. Marina, Ash and Ariel looked at Zak. He seemed absorbed in the flames.

'How do you know what's real, Zak?' said Marina. 'How do you know when something is right?'

As Zak turned to look at her, Marina gasped, feeling his eyes bore right into her mind. '*Is* this a game, Zak?' she whispered. 'Do you not value our friendship?'

Before he could answer, Ariel piped up. 'We'll be the only ones at school who will know about you.' When Zak turned to her and looked into her mind, Ariel looked right back into his. 'I can do that, too,' she said. She smiled as she saw Zak's look of surprise.

At that moment, Archie came bounding into the camp.

'Dad's coming!' said Flame, jumping up.

'Flipping heck,' said Ariel.

'Quick – sit down, Flame!' said Marina.

As Flame sat back in her chair, she saw that Zak had vanished.

'What on earth are you all doing up at this time?' said Colin, walking towards them with a torch.

'We're just talking, Dad,' said Ash with a smile. 'Come and sit down,'

Colin laughed. 'You never "just talk" – you're usually arguing. And anyway, it's late and you should be asleep by now.'

Flame's heart missed several beats. Where was Zak? Had her father seen him? She looked towards the Wild Wood, but all was dark and still. 'You've got a lovely fire there,' her father was saying as she turned back to the campfire.

'So what have you been talking about then?' said Colin, sitting down on the chair that only moments before Zak had occupied.

Ariel grinned. 'Magic.'

'Ah. I wondered if that would surface again.'

'The Sprites are an amazing family, don't you agree, Dad?' said Ariel.

Colin smiled. 'Yes, they are.' The girls waited for their father to ask them questions about their magic power, but he seemed content to watch the flames.

After a few minutes, Ariel said, 'Dad, if you had to tell us four things we should remember – you know, things we should do in our lives – what would they be?'

'Like life rules, you mean?'

Ariel nodded. Colin thought for a moment, then said, 'Be honest, be kind, work hard and smile. Will that do?'

The sisters all laughed.

'That's perfect, Dad,' said Ariel.

'Now come on, it's time you went to bed,' said Colin.

Ten minutes later, the campfire was doused and the sisters were all tucked into their sleeping bags in the caravan.

As they lay in the darkness, Ariel said, 'Do you think we're safe from Zak now?'

Flame yawned. 'Yes, I think so – or at least for the time being.'

'Do you think he's all bad?'

'I don't know,' said Flame. 'I don't think he knows.'

'Nobody is all bad,' said Marina.

'So says Saint Marina, Saviour of Wayward Boys,' said Ash.

Ariel said, 'Well, anyway, it's nice to be out here again, all together.'

As the Sprite Sisters fell into a deep sleep, the boy with hawk-like eyes picked up his bicycle from the flinty track and rode home.

THE END

SPECIAL THANKS

With thanks to my editor, Alison Pressley, for her wonderful support and astute comments.

With thanks to Chris Winn for his striking cover illustration, the Sprite Towers map and the Circle of Power diagram.

With thanks to Simon Cheshire for his clear, professional advice on self-publishing, and for designing and formatting the text.

With thanks to Matthew Johnson of Starfish, designer of my lovely website.

Thanks also to my friends, Patricia Mullin and Vicky Manthorpe, and to my son, Alex, for their critical help and support.

Lastly, a big 'thank you' to all my readers! Happy Spriting!

ABOUT THE AUTHOR

Sheridan Winn lives in Norfolk and has
two grown-up children.
The eldest of four sisters, she grew up in
a big country house surrounded by trees.
She likes walking as she finds it a good
way to think up ideas for her stories.
Since she was a child, she has written
a diary every day, and wherever she
goes she carries a notebook and a pen.
At night, she keeps them beside her,
in case she wakes up with a good idea.

Find out more about Sheridan and
The Sprite Sisters and send her your
comments at: www.sheridanwinn.com

HAVE YOU READ ALL
THE SPRITE SISTER STORIES?

1) THE CIRCLE OF POWER

Each of the Sprite Sisters has a magical power related to one
of the four elements – Fire, Water, Earth and Air. When Ariel
discovers her power on her ninth birthday, their circle is complete.
The girls' magic must be kept secret, and used only for good.
If not, the consequences could be dire.

The Sprites' big house in the country is full of laughter and
sunshine, but a shadow is falling. Everything the Sprite Sisters
hold dear will soon be shattered by the arrival of someone who is
intent on destroying their power …

2) THE MAGIC UNFOLDS

The Sprite Sisters' home, Sprite Towers, is under threat. The roof
is leaking and their enemy, the ruthless Glenda Glass, is
determined to have the house for herself. Tensions are mounting
between the girls as they prepare for the most important concert
of their lives. Can the Sprite Sisters resolve their differences
and summon all their magic powers to save Sprite Towers?

3) THE SECRET OF THE TOWERS

The summer holidays bring campfires and new-found freedom to
the Sprite Sisters. When they find the key that promises to unlock
the secret of Sprite Towers, it seems that the magic of the old
house is about to be released. But danger is lurking in their midst.
Are the Sprite Sisters' powers strong enough to save them from
the dark magic used by another side of the family?

4) THE GHOST IN THE TOWER

When the ghost of Glenda Glass's wicked ancestor Margaret is released, the atmosphere at Sprite Towers gets decidedly chilly, and the Sprite Sisters' Hallowe'en party turns far more sinister than anybody had planned. Only the sisters can rid Sprite Towers of the phantom. And that means entering the portal in the tower and risking their lives to change the past …

5) NEW MAGIC

When the Sprite Sisters' distant cousin, Verena Glass, inherits the magic power of the Sprite family, her evil grandmother Glenda Glass sees a way to get rid of the Sprite Sisters once and for all. A deadly battle begins as Glenda pushes her granddaughter towards using dark power. Flame, Marina, Ash and Ariel will only be free if they solve the mystery of the Crossed Circle – but that means trusting Verena …

THE SPRITE SISTERS
Four sisters
Four elements
Four powers

THE SPRITE SISTERS
Four sisters
Four elements
Four powers

Lightning Source UK Ltd.
Milton Keynes UK
UKOW030718010312

188120UK00004B/7/P